PASSAGEWAYS

PASSAGEWAYS

A SHORT STORY COLLECTION

VALERIE D. GRAY · LISA MICHELLE HESS · PETER LEAVELL · REBECCA CAREY LYLES

REBECCA CAREY LYLES, EDITOR

PERPEDIT ✓ PUBLISHING, INK

Passageways: A Short Story Collection

Perpedit Publishing, Ink
PO Box 190246
Boise, Idaho 83719
perpedit.com

These stories are works of fiction. Names, characters, places and incidents are either the products of the authors' imaginations or are used fictitiously.

First eBook Edition: 2014
First Paperback Edition: 2014

ISBN 978-0-9894624-3-3 (eBook)
ISBN 978-0-9894624-2-6 (Paperback)

Cover by Koeber Designs / koeberdesigns.com
Image of girl by Melissa Rose Boord

Published in the United States of America
Perpedit Publishing, Ink

CONTENTS

CONTENTS (CONT'D)

EDITOR'S NOTE

For the past several months, I've been privileged to work with good friends, who also happen to be good writers, to create this compilation for your reading pleasure. The stories are as varied as the authors, yet they all address transition. We write about movement, whether from place to place, emotion to emotion, or from one way of thinking to another.

Lisa Michelle Hess, assistant editor for *Passageways*, says, "Enlightenment comes when we're willing to dwell for a time in the spaces between—in the passageways of life."

Come dwell with us, if only for a time.

Rebecca Carey Lyles
Editor, Passageways

This book is dedicated to our families
who never stop believing in us and our writing.
Bless you for your encouragement and your patience
with our long hours at the computer.

The life of every man is a continued chain of incidents, each link of which hangs upon the former. The transition from cause to effect, from event to event, is often carried on by secret steps, which our foresight cannot divine, and our sagacity is unable to trace.

JOSEPH ADDISON, ENGLISH ESSAYIST, POET,
PLAYWRIGHT AND POLITICIAN, 1672-1719

PASSAGEWAYS

A SHORT STORY COLLECTION

MATTIE CUMMINS

Rebecca Carey Lyles

Mattie Cummins looked both ways before she slid her hand into her coat pocket. The weapon was still there. She'd checked before entering the building, but knowing it remained within easy reach was crucial to her mission.

Seventeen days had passed since her last conquest, leaving her desolate and hollow, a mere shell of a woman. Today would change everything. She stroked the sleek metal, strengthened and reassured by its solid curves. Her breath evened out, and two-and-a-half weeks of tension drained from her shoulders.

Mattie removed her hand from her pocket. No more pacing her two-room flat. No more sleepless nights. No more denying herself. Tonight, she would celebrate. She'd eat that last slice of chocolate bar, the one she'd purchased a month ago and cut into seven precise pieces, God's number for perfection.

Just thinking of the Swiss confection made her mouth water. She swallowed and with soundless steps began to weave her way through the cavernous building. Her plan had been to treat herself to a chocolate slice following each victory and to finish the candy bar within two weeks, three at most.

The first week, she'd had one glorious triumph after another. Not bad for a sixty-seven-year-old, never-been-dependent-on-a-man single woman. It was while piece number six was melting on her tongue seventeen days ago that she'd planned her next move and dared to dream of her next reward. A jelly roll, perhaps?

But, the best-laid plans of mice and men... Mattie pressed her lips together. She'd pushed her luck by gazing too far into the future without a crystal ball. That's what her Grandmother Matilda would have said. Mattie scratched the underside of her nose with her knuckle. And then Great-Aunt Rena Mae, her grandmother's sister, would have added her two bits. "The book of Proverbs talks about a woman who *laughed* at the future, Matilda."

Whenever her great-aunt mentioned the laughing woman, her grandmother's quick retort was always the same. "The only laughable thing anyone can know about the future, Rena Mae, is there'll be plenty more crackpots just like that batty lady in the Bible." Mattie sighed. Her elderly caretakers had argued about everything.

As she neared her target, her heart began to drum her ribs and her palms grew moist. She squared her shoulders, determined to complete her mission. This was what she'd been waiting for. She mustn't panic.

For two weeks, her career had been stymied. First, a vagrant whose grease-rimmed hat only partially covered his long stringy hair had hijacked the corner across from her building. Propped against the neighboring apartment house, he strummed a battered guitar and greeted passersby from dawn to dusk every day. She, for one, ignored him.

It was bad enough the neighborhood troublemakers sprawled on the curbs spouting vile language and blasting loud music on those boom-box things. Now, a strange, dirty, brazen man had joined them. She'd gotten nowhere with her landlord when she complained about the hoodlums. And when she asked him to call the police to report the bum, he'd said she could call them herself or discuss the matter with the other building's manager.

Right then, before her nerve failed her, Mattie had marched directly from his office to the street corner and pushed the "walk" button. While she waited for the light to change, the haunting strains of a harmonica rose between passing cars. She located the source of the music, saw the tramp had an instrument at his mouth, and frowned. Just because he had an ear for melody didn't make him safe. After all, he was a man.

When the light turned green, and the pedestrian signal began to blink its countdown, she scurried across the street, grateful she was wearing her longest skirt and the wind wasn't blowing. Her grandmother had warned her men sometimes faked disabilities and stooped to begging so they could peek up women's dresses. She hugged her ribs and avoided eye contact, even though the man was playing *Danny Boy*, her grandmother's favorite ballad. Although she'd never tell the beggar, the melody was especially beautiful coming from a harmonica.

In all her forty-one years in the neighborhood, she'd never before entered the other apartment building. The office was just inside the door, and a notice on the window told her the manager, a Mr. Barinski, was out of town. All inquiries should be directed to the regional management company.

Mattie frowned, shoved her fists into her coat pockets and reread the notice. The out-of-state prefix meant she couldn't contact the company. Her telephone plan was limited to local phone calls. Even if she'd had friends and relatives in another town, her pension didn't allow for extravagances like long-distance conversations.

She'd exited the building to the sound of *Amazing Grace*, which just happened to be her great-aunt's most beloved hymn, and chanced a glance at the man huddled against the wall. How did he know? Before she could look away, he'd winked at her. From then on, she'd only ventured outside when he was absent from the corner.

Mattie shuddered and held her cheeks, which were hot with the memory of that humiliating encounter. Such impudence. Her grandmother was right.

But the bum wasn't her only impediment. Her second roadblock had come in the form of snoops with furrowed foreheads and prying eyeballs who'd spied on her every move, ogling her like she was a common criminal—which, of course, she wasn't. She was a female William Wallace.

Mattie closed her eyes and pictured her handsome hero. Oh, how she loved that *Braveheart* movie. Like the Scots, her townspeople needed her.

"Ma'am, are you okay?"

A young woman was standing between the cash register and the dressing room, her head cocked to the side and her thick eyebrows clumped like dueling hedges.

Mattie gave her a sideways glance.

The salesgirl stepped closer.

What was this? Another barrier? Mattie frowned. She'd waited too long to be thwarted again. "I'm..." She cleared her throat. "I'm fine. Just a little dizzy spell." She touched her temple for effect. Even if she wasn't actually nauseated, the girl's perfume was potent enough to make an elephant woozy.

"Oh, dear." The girl grabbed Mattie's arm. "You should sit down. We have a chair right over there."

Half-pulled, half-pushed toward the chair, Mattie stammered, "I don't..." Before she could finish her sentence, she was deposited on the padded seat.

"I'll get some water and be right back," the salesgirl said. "If you start to pass out, put your head between your knees."

The instant the pushy do-gooder rounded a corner, Mattie jumped to her feet. She had to act and act now. No perky size two with wayward eyebrows and cheap cologne was going to ruin her day. She wouldn't *dream* of sitting in the middle of a department store with her head hanging between her legs. How unladylike. Besides, she had work to do.

The sudden movement made her feel lightheaded, which was a bit of a relief. Her little white lie wasn't a lie after all. She hoped her great-aunt, who hated fibs and whose spirit surely inhabited her favorite store, understood what had just happened. Mattie clutched the back of the chair to steady herself, all the while hearing her grandmother's voice. "Time's a wastin', girlie, time's a wastin'."

Lifting her head, Mattie brushed frizzy gray curls from her eyes before she turned to stride in her no-nonsense leather walking shoes to where she'd been standing before she was so imprudently interrupted. Even if the girl had been sent to spy on her, Mattie Cummins would not be stopped. She'd do the job and zip onto the escalator before those snappy little high heels could tap-tap their way back to the women's department.

She glanced at where she'd last seen her target. Good, still there. Midafternoon was always the best time to work. She scanned the surrounding area. All clear. Grasping her weapon, she lifted it from the bottom of the big pocket, stepped closer, drew a stabilizing breath, took aim—and did it.

One snip of the fingernail scissors, and the sweater's spare button was hers. Mattie caught the plastic packet with her free hand and dropped it into her other pocket. With her lips clamped between her teeth to contain a shout, she hopped a tight circle between the clothing racks, her clenched fists and scissors raised above her shoulders.

When her victory dance wound down, she once again faced her target, a bulky gray-and-white striped button-down sweater. She caressed the top button. Its pearled luster glowed in the fluorescent lighting. What a beauty. The matching button in her pocket would be a marvelous addition to her quilt.

Mattie smiled. Nothing was sweeter than cuddling under the button quilt's cozy warmth with Sophronius, her cat. Sophro, who'd been named after Saint Sophronius of Jerusalem, her great-aunt's favorite saint, liked to sleep with her beneath the heavy blanket, but he hated to walk on the buttons. He'd lift his paws and hiss, even swat at the hard objects, obviously annoyed by the unpredictable surface.

After years of sewing one beautiful button at a time onto the flannel backing, she was pleased but sad she had room for only a few more. With the newest addition, the total count would be three-thousand, five-hundred and seventy-nine. Mattie pursed her lips. What would she do when she ran out of space? She could add more fabric, but it was getting so heavy.

"Oh, here you are." Ms. Eyebrows came scurrying toward her. "Sorry I didn't come right back with the water. I was waylaid by a..." The girl stared at the nail scissors in Mattie's hand. "What are you...?"

Mattie dropped the scissors into her pocket and adjusted her coat collar. "I know it's impolite to practice personal hygiene in public, but my fingernail snagged on this sweater, and I didn't want it to catch on the others." She prayed Great-Aunt Rena Mae hadn't heard her spew yet another untruth, one she'd practiced over and over for situations like this.

The salesgirl raised a thick eyebrow. "I carry a nail file for stuff like that."

"Oh, so do I. In my purse, which I forgot. Silly me." Oh, dear. Another fabrication. Sleep would be long in coming tonight.

"Well, here's your water. I need to get back to work. Just throw the cup in that trashcan over there when you're finished."

"Thank you, Miss..." Mattie snuck a peek at her nametag. "Abigail. I am quite grateful for your concern."

Abigail nodded and trotted away,

Mattie dropped her chin to her chest. Her pulse pounded in her ears, and she could feel sweat drip from her armpits down her sides. The odor of her fear mingled with the heady scent that permeated the girl's wake.

She blew out a long breath. That was a close one. Maybe she should find a new vocation.

But then... She scanned the brightly lit area with its smiling manikins and rack upon rack of colorful clothing. So many buttons. So many *beautiful* buttons. And the aroma. She sniffed and then sniffed again. Oh, how she loved the department store's fragrance, which always brought back memories of shopping with her grandmother and great-aunt.

She flipped through the other sweaters. Red buttons, yellow buttons, silver buttons. Mmm, here was a square copper-colored set. Delightful. She searched for a spare button but didn't see one. Oh, well. There'd be others.

Something crunched beneath her foot. Mattie bent down and picked up a packet of small buttons, at least five of them. Her knees popped as she stood, but she didn't mind. The collection reflected a dazzling rainbow of colors.

She examined her find. One button was broken. Not good. If only she'd known the packet was on the floor. Surely, she would have salvaged it.

"Miss Cummins, what have you got there?"

Mattie whipped around. A big bald man in a black uniform was staring at her, his beefy hands on his wide leather belt. His nametag declared him to be "Harold M. Security."

She shoved the buttons at him. "I found these on the floor just now, but I don't know what sweater they go to."

He snorted. "*Found* them, huh?"

Mattie narrowed her eyes. Was he accusing her of something? And how did he know her name?

"You seem to have a way of *finding* buttons." He snatched the packet from her fingers. "So, what'd you use to cut these loose?"

She raised her palms. "I didn't. I swear I didn't." Her voice quaked. "Cross my heart, hope to die, they were on the floor."

Harold M. Security shook the packet under her nose. "I want you to find the sweater these belong to and find it now. After that, we'll go to my office for a pat-down."

Mattie gasped and stepped back, knocking coats off their hangers. She grabbed one and reached for another.

"Stop."

She straightened, staring at the security guard, who puffed his chest and emphasized his words with staccato finger stabs. "Find–that–sweater–NOW, Matilda Lorraine Cummins."

Mattie dropped the coat. He knew her full name, but how? And why? With trembling hands, she slid one sweater after another across the bar, barely able to breathe. Although she scrutinized each garment, she didn't see any with buttons even remotely similar to the ones she'd found.

Harold M. Security folded his arms. "Okay, you're off the hook this time, but you know what this means?" He walked over to the trash can and tossed the packet in.

Mattie groaned. All those gorgeous buttons headed for the landfill.

He moved closer again, nose to nose.

Mattie tried to stand her ground, but his nearness was almost more than she could bear. Not only was his breath worse than her cat's, she'd never let a man get that close before.

"This means the person who bought the sweater will one day lose a button, maybe two—those overseas workers don't waste much thread on buttons these days.

But will that customer be able to replace missing buttons? Nooo. Why? Because *she didn't get spare buttons with her purchase.*"

He pointed at the garbage can. "Each garment in this store, Miss Cummins, has specially designed buttons unique to a specific article of clothing. Sure, the person who bought the sweater could sew on any old button, but that's not the point. Our customers buy designer garments with designer buttons. The cost includes the matching replacement buttons. They ought to be able to take those home with them." He squinted at her. "Don't you agree?"

Mattie managed a small nod. She hadn't thought of it that way before.

"And wouldn't you agree that if I had deposited those buttons in my pocket rather than throwing them in the trash, I would be stealing them?"

"But..." Her lips trembled. Throwing away perfectly good buttons was a terrible waste.

He tapped her collarbone. Mattie retreated into the coat rack again.

"Do you agree that taking buttons is thievery?"

She lowered her gaze. Ever since she was a child, she'd thought of extra buttons as, well, extras. Grandmother Jenkins had gone on and on about what a waste spare buttons were. They'd just get thrown away when a buyer took the dress or skirt or blouse home, filling garbage cans across the city and ultimately overflowing the landfill with plastic, which would not, *could not* decompose for thousands, maybe millions of years.

Great-Aunt Rena Mae would pat her agitated sister's arm. "Now, Matilda, you know God is going to destroy this old earth and create a new one someday soon. Don't let something as trivial as buttons raise your blood pressure."

Despite Rena Mae's admonition, Mattie had shouldered her grandmother's cause when she passed away. She considered herself a heroine, one who was doing a noble deed by using the buttons rather than leaving them for others to discard and banish to the city dump.

His finger was now at her nose. Mattie watched it jab with each word.

"Miss Cummins, answer–my–question."

She uncrossed her eyes. "Yes, Sir…Officer…" She would agree to anything he said, as long as it kept her out of his office. God only knew where all that patting would lead.

———

Mattie scurried past the vagrant, who was playing the guitar and singing a vaguely familiar tune. He interrupted his song to call, "Have a good evening," but she wasn't about to give him the satisfaction of a response.

Inside her apartment building, Mattie stomped the four flights to her flat. She'd encountered more than enough men for the day and she didn't care to chance riding an elevator with one right now. Harold M. Security hadn't frisked her, but he'd suggested, in so many words, that she not return to the store. Of all the nerve. She'd shopped there since she was a child. Who was he to deny her access?

At the top of the stairs, her elderly neighbor was sweeping dust bunnies into the hallway.

Mattie cringed. She didn't feel neighborly at the moment.

He nodded. "Good evening, Mattie."

"Hello, Gus."

He rested both hands on the broom handle. "How're you doing today?"

"Fine, thank you. And you?"

"Storm comin' in." Gus grimaced and grabbed his back. "My lumbago is acting up."

"Sorry to hear that." Mattie unlocked the door to her flat. Even before she turned the knob, she could hear Sophro yowling. She sighed. Yet another male to harass her. If she hadn't found him wandering in the alley half-starved when he was a kitten, she certainly would never have purposely acquired a tomcat.

"I'm coming. I'm coming." She pushed the door open. The big feline was seated in front of the refrigerator. Mattie removed her coat and hung it in the closet. "Enough, Sophro. I got your message, loud and clear."

After dinner, she turned off the lights, lit a candle and settled with Sophro and a cup of chamomile tea on the window seat. A library book lay on the cushion beside her, but tonight she couldn't read. The day had been long and hard—and she was weary.

She'd been so eager to sew another button onto the quilt. But after what happened at the store, she knew the button, which was still in her coat pocket, would be the final addition. Before she sewed it on, she'd have to rearrange some of the other buttons, so there'd be no bare spots.

Movement on the corner below her window caught her eye. She leaned forward. It was that beggar man again, dragging something. Why was he still there? Did he think he owned the corner or what? He passed under the streetlight, and she could see a crutch under one arm and what looked like a flattened cardboard box under the other. Working with one hand, he arranged the rectangle on the winter-brown grass, placing it next to the apartment wall.

One of the mangy dogs that prowled their neighborhood materialized in the lamppost's circle of light. She watched the man lie down on the cardboard and motion to the dog, which joined him on the makeshift mat. They nestled together in what looked like a familiar routine. The bum even wrapped his arm around the mutt.

Sophro climbed onto Mattie's lap and began to purr. Why hadn't she noticed the man and dog pairing up at night? She stroked her cat's soft fur. Could be she hadn't seen them because she closed the drapes when she switched on her lights, so the people who lived across from her couldn't see into her flat.

She moved the cat and her teacup and drew the curtains. Somehow, it felt like an invasion of privacy to watch a bum and a stray dog sleep, even though they were outside, where anyone could see them. She studied the clock. One-half hour until bedtime. If she hurried, she could complete the quilt.

Not that she felt like sewing. Tonight should have been an evening of celebration, yet she hadn't even bothered with the chocolate piece. This was a time to mourn, not rejoice. Her quilt had lost its luster—and she'd lost her purpose.

Pushing through the fog that threatened to smother her brain and shackle her body, she crossed the room to turn on the light and fumble in her coat pockets for the button and scissors. After retrieving her sewing basket from the top shelf of the closet, she sat down on the end of the bed. In the early years, she'd carried the quilt to the living area to sew on new buttons. But the blanket had gotten so heavy that nowadays she only moved it off the bed to change the sheets.

Sophro stepped over the buttons, snuffling and lifting his paws in disdain. Finally, he reached his objective, her pillow, and twisted into a tight ball on top of it. When he wrapped his paws around his eyes, Mattie shook her head. "Is it really that bad?"

What was supposed to require thirty minutes took almost two hours. Her back ached, her eyes hurt, and her fingers were stiff and sore. If she hadn't had to decide which buttons could be moved without leaving big gaps and what colors, sizes and shapes went best together, she might have made better progress. She wasn't totally satisfied with the final product, but at least she could say the quilt, which had been years in the making, was finished.

Mattie rubbed her eyes and yawned. Surely the achievement was worthy of that final piece of chocolate. But instead of jubilation, emptiness had once again invaded her soul.

———————

The next morning, Mattie woke to the raucous clang of her wind-up alarm clock. Although she'd tossed and turned for hours, she must have eventually fallen asleep. She tapped the off-button on the vibrating timepiece.

Sophro jumped to the floor. By the sound of his whiny meow, she knew he was irritated. He despised the alarm clock.

Mattie rolled to her back to stare at the ceiling. Why had she set the alarm to ring so early? Did she have a doctor's appointment this morning? No. A meeting with the pension office? No. Then she remembered. Shoving the covers aside, she grabbed her robe from the end of the bed and hurried to the big window to open the drapes.

The sun was peeking between the buildings. As far as she could see in the growing light, streets, bushes, buildings and vehicles were coated with a soft layer of white. Sunshine broke through the clouds and shimmered off the treetops. She smiled. After breakfast, she'd put a leash on Sophro and they'd go for a stroll. He didn't particularly enjoy walking in the snow, but she'd made him little booties that helped him tolerate the cold.

As if he knew what she was thinking, Sophro joined her on the window seat.

She looked down at the corner across the street. The man and the dog were gone. Maybe they'd found a warmer spot. She hoped so. She was about to turn away when the snow rippled and swelled, and the dog's head popped out. She jumped. "Oh, my, Sophro. That was a surprise."

The mongrel looked around before it lurched out of the snowdrift.

Sophro hissed and arched his back.

After a quick shake, the dog trotted up the street, illuminated by a shaft of sunlight that brightened the surrounding buildings. Movement on the corner caught Mattie's attention again. This time, she saw the vagrant's upper body slowly emerge from the snow. Even from four stories up, she could see his puzzled expression. Maybe he hadn't heard the forecast. He shook snow from his hat and jacket but stopped and seemed to be staring at his legs.

Finally, he raised his crutch and pulled to a standing position. Steadying his stance, he reached down and, with apparent effort, lifted something off the ground and wrapped it around his shoulders. Snow cascaded off in a whoosh of icy sparkles. Then, button after button caught the sunshine and refracted it to the waking world. Like a king decked out in a jeweled robe, the man stood tall and proud.

He turned his face to the sky. The wide, toothless grin that creased his thin cheeks warmed Mattie's heart. She couldn't hear him, but she could see his mouth move. *Thank you, thank you, thank you.*

She hugged her cat. "He likes it, Sophro. He likes the quilt."

Sophro patted her cheek with his paw.

"Ah, you're such a sweet kitty." Mattie set him on the seat and went to the cupboard. "This calls for celebration. Canned salmon for you, and Swiss chocolate for me."

Sophro licked his front paws, first one, then the other, purring louder than he'd ever purred before.

EIGHTEEN MINUTES

Peter Leavell

I twirled my hat on one finger before setting it on the seat. "Twentieth century now," I told my traveling companion, who sat across from me. "Trains cannot be late, and work cannot be missed."

"Aye, Mr. Ruddick." Mr. Derby reached into his vest pocket and pulled out a gold watch. "Durham to Darlington, thirty-two minutes."

I raised an eyebrow. "Not today."

He returned the timepiece to its pocket. "Not with your look-a-like standing on the platform three minutes late."

I frowned. The thought of having a double upset my sense of dignity.

"I say..." Mr. Derby lifted a finger. "Have you ever noticed how extraordinarily twin-like the two of you are. They say we all have a double out there somewhere."

"Preposterous." I sniffed and glanced out the window

to see the station pass from view. "Herby will make up the steam."

"And catch three minutes? I doubt it." Mr. Derby wiggled his mustache. "Weren't you thirty seconds late yourself?"

My dignity again. "Fashionably so."

"Quite right. Yes."

I eyed *The Times* next to him, but he evidently preferred to continue the conversation.

"Was it your wife again?"

I didn't reply. The train car's old-leather scent swirled around us, along with the not-so-pleasant mix of body odor and stale cologne.

He nodded knowingly. "My wife has troubled me of late, too. Let me ask you…" He clasped his hands. "Is there a way to buy food if one does not work for the funds?" Without waiting for my response, he answered his question. "No. To miss a minute, a second of work means less food on the table." He lowered his brow. "My wife understands none of this, says telling the children the same balderdash will only make them turn out like me. She talks as if my character has been flawed by my diligence." He crossed his arms. "Hmph."

I picked up my hat and rubbed lint off the crown with my sleeve. "I give my wife eighteen minutes a night of undivided attention for conversation."

"How generous."

"She wants more."

He blew a breath through his thick mustache. "I didn't know…" He shook his head. "My poor man."

"She asked me this morning…" I leaned closer and

lowered my voice. "She asked me not to work today."

His brow furrowed. "You've lost control."

And what little dignity I had. "I work. She doesn't. How can she understand?"

"My wife doesn't understand, either."

I placed my hat on my knee. "My wife is beautiful. I cannot deny it. But with beauty comes a price."

"Which is?"

"She bores me."

"Oi!" Mr. Derby jumped to his feet and stepped to the door of our private compartment. Through the window, I could see my double standing on the other side.

Mr. Derby yanked the door open. "We're steady fellows aboard this train." He stabbed his forefinger at the man's chest. "We've jobs, you see, and to keep them, we must be on time." His voice rose. "If all the trains were late, thanks to blokes like you, His Majesty's empire would crumble."

My double clenched his fists. "It was my wife, you see—"

"A wife is no excuse!" Mr. Derby slammed the door in the man's face and yelled through the glass. "Find another compartment. This one's full." He plopped back down in his seat and crossed his arms again. After a moment, he sighed, as if he was beginning to regret his words.

Time to bolster the man's dignity. "Well deserved," I said. "Spot on."

Silence regained its form. Branches slid along the side of the train as it passed through the forest. Their leaves glistened in the morning's bright sunlight. I rested my hands on my hat and attempted to prepare myself for the day ahead. My morning so far had been disconcerting, to say the least.

A figure flashed by the window.

I blinked and gasped.

Mr. Derby sat up. "My dear Mr. Ruddick, you've gone white."

"I..." Had I really seen what I thought I saw? "I think I saw someone fall from the train."

"Impossible." He craned his neck to look outside. "From the train, you say?"

The screech of metal against metal filled the air as the car lurched to a stop. My companion flew into my lap. I pushed him away and retrieved my crushed hat.

Seated once more, Mr. Derby combed his mustache back into place with his fingers, straightened his vest, and brushed the shoulders of his coat, apparently purging himself of the unpleasant experience.

I heard the sound of hurried footsteps and turned in time to see conductors charge through the corridor. I opened a window and leaned out to search for a body. The pungent cloud of coal smoke wafting from the engine made me cough. At the rear of the train, the conductors huddled in a mass of blue uniforms, but they soon separated and dispersed into a nearby thicket.

Beyond the engine, I saw a small station nestled between tall evergreens. The platform was filled with constables, who lined up as I watched and marched toward the train.

"What's the word?" asked Mr. Derby.

I sat back. "Village bobbies."

"What are they doing here?" He stuck his head out his

window. "Think they're looking for your train jumper?"

The thump of pounding feet again filled the passageway. I swiveled. This time, a familiar figure ran by. It was Rose, my wife! She was followed by two policemen.

I flung the door open and stepped into the passageway just as she disappeared through the exit at the end of a car, the constables close on her heels.

I ran after them onto the platform, but Rose was nowhere in sight. As I jumped to the ground, a bush rustled nearby. I stopped. From the branches crawled the man who resembled me, except his clothing was filthy, and he wore no hat. Two conductors came running to help him to his feet.

I started toward them but changed course when I heard a woman cry out. I hurried toward the sound and saw my wife on the other side of the train coupling, struggling to free herself from the constables who held her arms. I shouted, "Rose, what's going on?"

She paused, and the men took a better grip. My wife seemed surprised to see me. "Jasper."

I held out my palms. "What have you done?"

"I threw you from the train." She stared at my suit. "But you don't look as if you've tumbled."

"You threw me from the train?" Was she barmy?

My wife jutted her chin. "And I'd do it again."

I glanced at my double. He was arguing with conductors on my side of the track. "I did not jump," he insisted. "I was shoved!"

My dignity struggled with the shock of my wife's words. "You pushed the wrong man, Rose."

She shook her head. "That can't be. I was sure it was

you."

"Why?" I asked. "Why all the bother?"

The constables nodded and leaned closer. Obviously, they were as mystified as I was by her behavior.

Rose stared at the blue sky above us as if searching the heavens for an answer. Finally, she said, "You, my dear husband, are a bore."

Any pride I had left was squashed like a beetle under her shoe. I wanted to object. Yet, hadn't I felt the same for her?

But now, standing on a pine-scented hillside with a railroad track between us and dozens of passengers gawking from train windows, I saw my wife with new eyes. Her hair was disheveled, her gaze wild and fiery, her words fierce and angry. Rose was a different woman than the one who'd meekly asked me to stay home from work.

I chuckled. She piqued my interest. I liked it.

I smiled. "My dear..."

Rose cocked her head.

I pointed toward the station. "There is a tidy pub behind the station that serves a tolerable pint and manageable cold ham. Perhaps you'd be free to join me for a bite?"

"What of your work day?" She tried to pull away from the constables, but they held tight.

"Shipping will go on without me." I held out a hand.

The constables hesitated, but then one said, "All seems to be well," and they released her.

Rose approached the train, wrapped her skirt about her knees, and bent beneath the coupling. I offered my hand, all the while wondering if this wife of mine would accept assistance.

Once she was on my side, she said, "Thank you, dear," and grasped my arm. I helped her step from the railway bed to the lush green shoulder.

"That's her, that's the woman!" The voice came from behind us. "She's the one who knocked me from the train."

I spun and saw my double approaching. In an instant, conductors and constables circled the three of us, like hunting dogs surrounding a fox.

My double pointed at Rose. "You pushed me."

She wiped coal dust from her shoulder but didn't speak.

My dignity took a step forward, and I followed. "She meant to push me."

"But she shoved me off the blooming train."

I pulled my wife closer to my side. "An accident, to be sure." I glanced at the police. "Her wrath was meant for me, but I don't believe I will press charges."

Rose giggled under her breath.

With my arm tight around her, I pushed through the circle of men, ignoring my double, who continued to argue with police. In a train window just ahead, I saw Mr. Derby watching us. His brow was raised, his eyes were wide and his mouth gaped.

I shrugged with as much dignity as I could muster.

———————

A SMALL MISTAKE

Lisa Michelle Hess

One day, when I was very young and my brother barely more than a baby, he and I boarded the wrong bus. I don't think of that immediately, though, as I watch the scarlet points on each of Evie's cheeks seep across her face and converge with the red tide creeping up her neck.

Incensed by my audacity, she sputters, "But, but, when did you do that?"

"When I said I would, Evie." I form each word slowly, my tone carefully neutral. "I said I was going to make an appointment for the Playwell Company to talk to the city council about a new playground across from the diner." Before she can interrupt, I add, "It's just an informational session. We agreed I would set up the meeting. The following month I reported that I had scheduled it."

"Well, I wasn't at those meetings." Her voice is rising with her color.

I know I should keep my mouth shut, but I can't help

myself. "Actually, you haven't been at the last three meetings. But the information *was* in the minutes, and you *were* at the meeting where we all agreed we should pursue the idea of creating a playground on one of the vacant city lots. Then, we unanimously voted to do just that."

She sits back and glares at each of us seated around the table. Finally, her lethal gaze settles on me. The other board members look relieved.

I stare calmly back at her with a look that belies my rapidly beating heart and the sweaty fist I'm clenching under the table.

Her eyes narrow. "Everyone apparently forgot to tell you only the president of the board is allowed to make appointments with the city council."

The emotional journey I take from surprise and dismay through disappointment, anger and, finally, resignation is a fairly quick one. I'd been here before. But this time I'd gotten my hopes up, believing the need was so obvious and the project so non-controversial, we would surely sail smoothly to our goal and finally make a difference.

Evie is ignoring the fact that she was the one who set me on this course months ago. That she had at one time applauded my suggestion and voted along with the others to "pursue the idea" of a playground. *Pursue the idea*. I get it now.

She ignores these facts because she's changed her mind and she knows she can. This is *her* realm. Like the other small towns dotted throughout this rural galaxy of sage and dust and rocks, our community is a world unto itself, with its own customs, culture, authorities and hierarchies.

Most importantly, Evie is one of "the indigenous." And me? I've called this place home for a decade, and my family has lived in the region many more generations than hers has. In fact, my ancestors literally arrived in this country on the Mayflower. Still, I'm the alien here.

And I've broken one of the many unwritten laws passed down and buried among this town's citizenry like landmines for the unsuspecting: *Dream big, but never presume to turn those dreams into reality. Nothing ever changes here. And that's the way we like it.*

"Besides," Evie snaps, "I didn't receive any minutes."

I sigh. "I emailed them, like I always do."

Here she tosses her head, and the glint in her eye signals another victory. "Email…" She sniffs, dismissing the evidence with a wave of her hand. "I never check email."

I continue to try to reason with her, which only makes her angrier. Suddenly, I'm tired, and it's as if I'm watching myself from across the room. Evie's red face is turning purple, and I can see that my calmness, my continued politeness, as much as my transgression, is driving her crazy. I could start yelling and swearing and get in her face, and she would back down, which would mean a quick end to this argument and possibly even absolution.

In your face is how people communicate here. At the counter in the NAPA store, I hear the owner ask longtime customers, "What the f**k you want?" And the customers answer, "Well, I need your help about as much as I need another asshole, I'll tell you that."

My politeness exhausts Evie. Knowing her, she thinks I'm hiding something or I have some secret agenda I won't share with her. Here, people are only polite to those they dislike or don't know. I'm not better than they are, or above rough language. I just can't bring myself to talk that way. Perhaps it's the frowns I imagine on my ancestors' faces, from those Mayflower Separatists all the way to my recently departed mother. They would be so disappointed in me, and I just can't bring myself to disappoint, even to fit in.

It is here I remember that day so long ago, and I realize I've done it again. I've boarded the wrong bus.

The day is crystal clear, unusual in our rainy city. Paul and I run ahead of our siblings through the bright morning sunlight. Laughing, we race each other to the bus stop. There we will wait with our older brother and sister for the city bus that delivers us to the private school we attend on the other side of town. We get to the stop well ahead of the others.

We barely have time to catch our breath before a bus swerves to the curb and rolls to a stop in front of us, belching diesel. The air brakes blast and the doors slide open. Like we always do, like we've been taught, I climb onto the bus and carefully deposit my paper ticket through the slot in the box beside the driver. Paul follows, high-kneeing his way up the steep steps on his short little legs, and we quickly find seats.

But unlike every day before this one, our siblings do not climb onto the bus behind us. They are too far away for the driver to even notice them. To our horror, the doors crash shut and the bus lurches forward.

Paul and I turn in panic to stare behind us through the scratched and dirty window for some glimpse of our brother and sister. I see them stop, in shock, I suppose, and then run toward the bus. But they are too late.

The other women at the table watch Evie and me spar. Their eyes are wide, their lips parted, and their attention swivels between us as we volley back and forth. The expressions on their faces would appear blank to the untrained eye, but I can see embarrassment on some, a pout of boredom here, a glint of defensiveness there and, above all, a desperate desire for us to *move on*.

Their main goal, I know, is to avoid being drawn into the argument. They're afraid of guilt by association and that the endless recriminations I'll suffer for my infraction will also be directed at them. They want, most of all, to pretend this unexpected ripple never ruffled the familiar surface of their lives.

Jane, who sits beside me, is particularly good at maintaining a maddening neutrality. If these meetings were the only place I'd encountered her, I would believe her to be ineffectual, simply attending to get out of the house. But this is not the case. Jane is, in fact, a force of nature. Like me, she has dreams of her own but followed her husband and his career and ended up in this place a decade ago.

Looking around as we drove into town, we'd both shaken our heads and said the same words to our husbands. "Two years. Two years, at the most." But we'd been lulled, like visitors to Brigadoon. The seduction was due to many things—small-town hominess, cheap real estate, the ever-changing light on the rocks, a full moon's ribbon reflected on the lake's mahogany ripple, the stillness, the cerulean sky. But mostly, having come from large cities, we were drawn in by our perception of its relative safety. This would be a good place to raise children.

When it comes to children, Jane has me beat. Her faith encouraged her to birth numerous children, and although still in her forties, she's on the verge of ushering the last one into adulthood. I'm relatively sure she's the designated queen among her fellow believers, and I do not begrudge her that status. She deserves it.

Jane has eight children. I have two. The watching part of me wonders, even as the other part of me continues to wrestle with Evie, whether or not I could have brought myself to have more children if, like Jane, I believed doing so would enhance my eternal reward.

Really, two was all I'd ever wanted, and I am happy with my boys. But as I consider Jane, I also think, not without guilt, that just one more would have been nice. A daughter would have been nice.

Jane sees me watching her and casually leans her elbow on the table. She subtly blocks the side of her face with her hand and rolls her eyes in response to Evie's continuing tirade. I will love her forever for that show of solidarity. I imagine us as allies who show the indigenous that change can be good. Together, we could help them understand life is not static. Things either improve or get worse, and things in this town haven't improved for quite some time.

But my fantasy is brief. Jane's husband is due to retire any day now from the government installation where all our husbands work. Then, their children raised and gone, they will also leave.

My brother and I go from panic to despair when the bus

turns where it's never turned before. Paul realizes as I do that not only are we alone, we are lost. Though paralyzed with fear, I sense my world begin to shift.

As the third of four children, the lines of defense between me and danger consist of family members. First, I have my father, who is unfalteringly fair, steady and faithful. After him is my mother who, from a combination of enthusiasm, literature and her astounding imagination, spins adventure for us under sheet-swathed tables, ensuring we never become bored and are never tempted to wander too far from home.

Next is the oldest child, my sister, who is the smartest, most confident, most beautiful person I have ever known. Finally, I have my older brother, my hero who tortures me mercilessly but who, I am certain, would sacrifice his life to protect me. Through these multi-layers, no hint of peril has a chance to disturb Paul and me. We are protected, even spoiled, some would say. But to us, this is just the life we've always known, a life filled with love and safety we never question.

Paul looks up at me with big blue eyes that match my own. There is no trust in those eyes. He knows I'm not up to this task, that I cannot save us. I see no hint of hope in his baby face—only terror, and his fear makes me feel protective of him for the first time in my life. Slowly the realization that I am not just the third child, but another layer in the line of defense, settles on my shoulders. I'm so far down in the hierarchy, I never should have been called upon, but here I am.

I think of the heroes and heroines from all those stories our mother read us, Bible stories and family histories about brave pilgrims and pioneers, and a part of me realizes those stories weren't just for our entertainment. They were also *my mother's way of preparing me for a world where bad things happen, decisions have to be made, and people must act courageously.*

But she'd also instructed us to, "Never leave your seat until the bus stops. Never talk to strangers."

The bus rumbles on through neighborhoods I've never seen toward the center of the city. Barely breathing, I grasp Paul's small, sweaty hand and reach for the pole beside my seat. "It's all right," I tell him. "We're getting off."

Evie has calmed just a bit. "Who do you think you are?"

She doesn't say it in exactly those words. But her expression does. The derision, the anger, the smile that somehow manages to resemble a sneer. *That's not how we do things. You will never be one of us. We don't want your kind here.*

I think, sadly, *I loved you*. And I did, especially after the sudden loss of my mother. I threw myself into my infatuation with this town that would keep my children safe from the rest of the world, as if it could keep them from the hurt and the pain I'd suffered following her death. The way I felt was almost romantic. I loved the people here like a new wife loves a husband and throws herself into making a life for the two of them. She ignores his faults, the little hurts, and smothers him with her overwhelming need to create a perfect, unassailable nest.

The fantasy worked for a while. This small place was perfect for my small children, for the simple, small life I wanted for them. The traffic was so light they could ride their little bikes in the street. The park with its tiny crop of trees was to them the "Grassy Meadow" and the "Big Woods." Mayberry and Disney combined, the town was all the adventure they needed. They, themselves, were all the adventure I'd wanted, and all I could see.

Those times when I returned to the city with its smog and traffic and crime to visit my sister and brothers, I'd feel warm gratitude toward this place that would let my children grow in its small, safe womb. But my sons are getting older, standing on the precipice of their teen years. I've discovered there are two ways for an adolescent to react to life here. They either outgrow its confines and throw them off, or they remain small, like their environment.

I didn't create my boys to stay small. They have big dreams. They want to be the heroes of their own stories. They don't know it yet, but I've begun to feel a creeping dread that what they want, what they need, isn't possible in this town. If we stay, will they drown their dreams in 24-ounce cans of Canadian beer and promiscuous sex, like so many of their slightly older peers? I look into Evie's closed-off, bitter face and see their future. Involuntarily, I shudder, which makes her falter, for just a second.

My current experience in this town resembles a relationship after some years have passed, when you can no longer ignore the faults, yet you still see the potential. You long for your love to fulfill the possibilities you see, and you think, fatally, that you can help them get there.

The last time I visited the city, I went alone, without the children. Much to my surprise, it was again the city I loved. Astonished, I found myself embraced by long unobserved beauty and whispered memories. I stayed in the heart of it and, yes, there was too much traffic and graffiti and garbage reeking in back alleys. Everywhere I looked, conspicuous consumers hurried past the deranged, the sad and the poor as if they didn't exist.

But I also saw my childhood of museums and theaters, good food and coffee, bookstores and art, old friends and family, and a shared history. The city was wealthy with variety and bold creativity, a place so old and so big I could never make even the slightest mark on it for good or ill. I could go to the supermarket, the bank, the gas station every day for a year and never see one person who knew me or cared about me. So, why, in that huge, impersonal city, did I feel like I belonged in a way I've never felt in this small town?

Paul and I sway on shaky legs just behind the driver. I try to sound confident. "We need to get off."

"Huh?" His voice is gruff.

How can I muster the courage to speak again? "We need to get off." I yell in his ear to be sure he hears me above the rattling roar of the engine. "We're on the wrong bus!"

I am overjoyed when he pulls the bus over. Right now, right here, with no bus stop in sight. He comes to a quick halt that throws us forward, and we grab the fare box to keep from crashing into the windshield.

The look he turns on me is angry at first. But then, his eyes soften. "You meant to get on the 20?" As if by magic, he produces a sheaf of transfer tickets and a hole punch from somewhere about his waist.

I am so relieved I feel faint, but I manage a nod.

He punches two of the transfer tickets and hands them to me, then gestures behind us, using the hole punch like a pointer. "Go back that way and around the corner. You'll see the stop. Number 20 is right behind me. I'll call the driver and tell him to wait for you."

I whisper a "thank you" he probably can't hear and drag

Paul behind me down the steps and into the sun. "We have to hurry," I say to my brother and take off, pulling him behind me. "Run, Paul." We round the corner. I see the orange-and-white stop sign and the bus next to it with the number "20" on the front.

Panting, we climb onto the bus, the right bus. I scan the riders, hoping to see my big sister and brother. But they aren't there. I sit in the first open seat, and Paul settles in beside me. He still grasps my hand, but he has remained dry-eyed and reasonably calm throughout the entire ordeal. I smile down at him. He returns my smile with a look that is equal parts relief and triumph, and I realize I must have the same expression on my face.

The first thing I see as the bus pulls to the stop across from our elementary school is my mother. She's staring at the grimy bus windows with wide, searching eyes. I wonder, as Paul and I walk slowly toward the door, will she cry? Will she hug me too tight? Will she tell us how naughty we've been, how much we've made her worry?

Whoosh, the door opens, and we stumble down the steps into her arms. For a minute, she does hug us too tight. But then she pulls me back, looks me over at arm's length, and smiles. "Well, that was an adventure, wasn't it?"

Evie has gotten to the part where she says she knew this would happen, that she just can't work with me. One of us will have to resign.

I realize now that in their small wisdom, they've been right all along. I don't belong here, and neither do my children. I've never really wanted what they want. I tried to make their smallness into my safety, another line of defense, and that was unfair of me.

I see myself through Evie's eyes, and I understand her anger. I'm angry at myself, but only for an instant, because I know what to do next. She stops midsentence as I rise and make my way around the table to where she's standing, towering over all of us.

She flinches as I move toward her. Another woman gasps. They can't believe our disagreement has come to *this*.

I pull Evie to me and hug her tight. An eerie quiet settles on the room. I think the others have all stopped breathing. I know Evie has. Her body remains stiff and unyielding.

I don't care anymore that she doesn't want to understand and never will. "It'll be all right," I say softly. "I'm getting off now."

I wink at Jane's bewildered expression as I turn toward the exit. The quiet is broken, and everyone starts talking at once. I hear one of them call my name, followed closely by Evie's hard voice. "Let her go."

Whoosh, the door opens, and I step out.

JOHN WAYNE LIVES

Valerie D. Gray

Noreen eased the old Cadillac onto the freeway and glanced over at her father-in-law, who sat in the passenger seat, jiggling his legs. She patted his arm. "Relax, Dad. We'll be there in half an hour. Let's listen to some music." She found a station on the radio that was playing oldies. Maybe that would calm him.

He glowered at the car ahead of them. "If I ever find out who stole my winnings...well, they just better hope I don't."

"What winnings?" Noreen knew he was talking about the scam letter he kept in his wallet, but she couldn't think of another way to respond. She signaled a lane change and merged into the center lane.

He pulled his billfold from his back pocket, retrieved the tattered paper and carefully unfolded it. "This says I won the lottery...a hundred–thousand–dollars." He pursed his lips. "I'll know who stole my money when I see them driving a shiny new Cadillac."

Dropping the paper, he peered around the interior of the car as if seeing it for the first time. "Like this one..." He ran a bony finger over the dashboard, down the glove box and across the upholstered door panel.

"Dad, you know this was my father's car. Don't you just love the leather smell and how soft the upholstery feels?" She stroked the seat between them. "In case you forgot, this car is thirteen-years old."

He huffed. "Doesn't look it." Without warning, he upped the radio volume. "Quiet, we have to listen to this."

The commercial blasted so loud Noreen's eardrums vibrated, but she forced a smile. "Oh, a John Wayne Film Festival." She turned down the sound. "I'll make sure you get to watch it." Her father-in-law loved John Wayne movies.

But instead of being pleased, he groaned. "Did you hear what they said? They talked about the Duke like he's dead." He clutched the top of his head.

Noreen wondered if he was trying to keep it from blowing off. She flipped the blinker again. "Here's our off-ramp." She maneuvered into the exit lane.

"I'm gonna write me a letter," he declared. "Those people will get a piece of my mind." His blue eyes widened. "He isn't dead. I saw him on television yesterday. If John Wayne were dead, which he's not, he'd be rolling in his grave."

Jaw clamped, he opened the glove box and dug around inside it. "Here's a pen. Honey, do you have a piece of paper? I'll insist they make a public apology to the Duke and all his fans." He closed the glove box and picked up the letter he'd dropped. "This doesn't look important. Do you mind if I use it?"

"No, go ahead." Noreen waited for the light at the base of the ramp to change. Whatever it took to make him forget the sweepstakes.

Using his knee for a table, her father-in-law scribbled frantically on the blank side the paper, vocalizing every word. "Dear Sirs... How dare you have a commercial that insinuates the death of John Wayne. I'm sure he's as mad as I am, or madder." The car bumped over a manhole cover, causing him to punch a hole in the paper, but that didn't seem to faze him.

"I request an apology be aired on this radio station," he continued, "to the Duke and his family, friends, and fans." He held up the note. "Does that sound right? I'm so mad at them."

Noreen nodded, her focus on the traffic as she navigated a busy intersection.

He snorted. "I can't believe anyone would do that to him. John Wayne will no doubt sue them." For a long moment, he glared at the radio. Then he folded the paper and put it in his shirt pocket.

Noreen smiled. With any luck, the letter would still be there when she did the laundry, and she could toss it—or better yet, shred it. She slowed to enter the V.A. hospital's parking lot. What should she do? Tell her father-in-law his hero was dead, or leave it alone? "Um, Dad?"

"What, honey?" He sounded worried. "Something wrong?"

She pulled into a parking space, switched off the engine and turned to him. "Yes, Dad, there is something wrong."

He lifted his chin, as if bracing himself for the worst.

"Go ahead. Tell me. What's happened?"

She looked into his blue eyes. "Well, you know you're going to have some tests today to see how well your mind is working. Right?"

He nodded, and she saw moisture gather in the corners of his eyes.

"They won't hurt you." Offering him a gentle smile, she added, "but they're going to ask you a bunch of questions about life and facts about the date, the year, the president...things like that."

He sunk into his seat, drawing his chin in like a turtle retreating into its shell. "Are they going to ask me about John Wayne?"

"No, probably not." She took his wrinkled hand in hers. "But you're very upset about John Wayne, aren't you?"

"You bet!" He raised his bushy eyebrows. "I'm gonna write them and give them what for." Pulling his hand away, he began to knead his legs. "Can I use the typewriter when I get home?"

"Sure, but there's something you should know before you send the letter." She studied his face. His brow was furrowed and he was breathing hard. "Maybe we should cancel your appointment. I think you may be too upset to go through testing today."

"Doll, it takes too long to get appointments in this place. Let's just get it over with." He crossed his arms. "Tell me what you're going to tell me."

Noreen took a breath, praying, *God help him*. "It's about John Wayne."

"What about him?"

"He died." There, she'd said it.

His mouth dropped open. "No, not John Wayne!" Tears pooled in his eyes. "When? Tell me when."

She couldn't help it. She started to cry, too. "I'm not sure, but it was some time ago. Maybe twenty years." Oops. Had she said too much? She clamped her lips together, forbidding anything else to come out.

"This can't be true." He sniffed. "How'd he die?"

Noreen found a tissue in her purse and blew her nose. "Cancer, I think."

"Tell me it's not true. Please, *please* tell me it's not true." But then he stopped. "Am I that far gone?"

Noreen felt terrible for breaking her father-in-law's heart, but before she could respond, he bowed his head. After several minutes, she tapped his shoulder. "Dad, we have to get to your appointment. Are you ready?"

He blinked and looked around. "Oh, we're at the V.A. already. Did I sleep all the way here?"

"Some. You mostly listened to the radio and dozed off and on. It's hard not to fall asleep in these comfortable seats."

"Yep, this is some car your dad gave you." He released his seatbelt. "Okay, let's go. What are they doing to me today, do you know?"

"They're going to ask you a few questions, that's all."

"Let's get going, darlin'." He opened the car door. "There's a John Wayne festival this afternoon, and I don't want to miss it. That man is the greatest actor alive today."

———

MORNING SONG

Rebecca Carey Lyles

Charlie took one sip of the coffee, plopped the cup down and fumbled through the red plastic basket stuffed with cream and sugar packets. He'd never been fond of restaurant coffee, but this stuff was extra bitter. Muttering under his breath, he picked out a couple packets and tore off the ends. Mamie's coffee didn't need doctoring, not even when they were first married.

Stirring the white crystals into the coffee, he watched the mixture mellow into a milk-chocolate swirl. Soon, he no longer saw the cup or the café. Instead, he saw Mamie in the morning, her soft face creased by pillow lines. She bustled about their cozy kitchen, humming as she worked and struggling to restrain her eagerness for the new day until he'd downed his first cup of coffee and ceased his monotone grumbling.

Mamie opened the oven and pulled out a tin of muffins. She arranged the muffins in a small basket and set in front of him, along with butter and jam, just as the coffee finished perking. After filling his mug, she handed it to him with a shoulder squeeze and a kiss on his cheek. Then she went back to frying bacon.

Holding the cup with both hands, Charlie inhaled the warm, rich scent of her special blend while he waited for it to cool. As always, he marveled at her efficiency as she segued from lifting bacon from the skillet to cracking eggs into it without a moment's pause.

Although her cheerful smile never left her face, Mamie didn't say anything. She'd learned early in their marriage it took half a cup to make him civilized. At least that's what she said.

He chuckled and reached for her.

"Sir?"

Charlie blinked. The waitress had returned, this time with a plate of food in her hand.

"Oh, pardon me." He pulled back his hand. Thank God he hadn't grabbed the woman. "My mind must have been elsewhere."

"That's okay." Crow's feet accentuated her kind eyes. "It's a beautiful Colorado morning—springtime in the Rockies, as the song goes. Isn't that when the poets say our minds tend to wander?"

He moved the newspaper he'd been reading aside.

She lowered the plate to the paper place mat. "Eggs, toast and hash browns. Can I bring you anything else?"

"A glass of orange juice. This coffee is terrible."

"Oh, dear." She frowned. "I must have done something wrong."

"Sorry." Charlie cursed his crabbiness. Just because Mamie put up with his surly attitude didn't mean this

[44]

woman had to.

She slid a stray salt-and-pepper curl behind her ear. "I don't drink coffee, and neither did my husband, so I'm a novice at coffee-making. But I thought it was something simple I could do without bothering the cook." She sighed. "Evidently not."

Charlie shook his head. "I shouldn't be such a grouch."

"Don't apologize. I've got to learn how to make it right. Is it too weak or too strong?"

He couldn't help but smile at the determined woman. "Too strong. I don't know much about making coffee, either, but I think you could have measured wrong, or maybe it's been sitting a while."

"Let's see." One finger on her chin, she stared at the ceiling. Charlie noted the absence of a wedding ring. "I suppose I started perking it around five." She looked at him. "Has that been too long?"

He checked his watch. Eight twenty-three. "Yes, and then some." He grinned. "The longer coffee sits, the more bitter it tastes."

"Oh, my. Well, if nothing else, I learned something today." She patted his arm. "Thank you for your candidness."

The waitress turned to walk away but stopped. "Do you eat breakfast here often?"

He nodded. "Fairly often."

She cocked her head to the side. "If you come back tomorrow morning about the same time, I'll start a fresh pot at seven forty-five and give you a free cup just to show my appreciation. Sound like a good deal?"

"Sure does. I'll be here." The twinkle in her brown eyes

awakened his spirit like nothing else had since Mamie's death.

Later, when she handed him the bill, Charlie said, "I don't think I've seen you in here before."

"Probably not. This is only my third day."

He raised an eyebrow. "You seem new to this kind of work. If you don't mind me asking, what made you choose waiting on tables?"

She scraped at a spot on the table with her fingernail. "My, my husband..." She stopped, took a breath and started again. "My husband, Rich, died ten months ago. I'm still trying to adjust to life without him." She drew a ragged breath. "I thought this would get me out of the house and force me to be with people, help me to..."

Tears pooled in her eyes. "To get back into life." She grabbed his plate and bolted for the kitchen.

Charlie sighed, folded the newspaper and rolled it into a tight cylinder. He had work waiting for him at the office, but he couldn't bring himself to face it just yet. For a long time, he remained in his seat, staring out the window and tapping the paper in his palm.

———————

The sweet aroma of warm cinnamon rolls mingled with that of sizzling sausage, bacon and eggs greeted Charlie the next morning. Although he didn't see his new friend, the table where she'd waited on him yesterday was empty. Feeling a surprising sense of satisfaction with life, he pulled out a chair, sat down and opened his newspaper. Concentration was difficult. Even so, he resisted the urge to look for the waitress.

She approached the table while he was still reading

the front page. Her smile was again gracious, but her eyes were serious. "I owe you an apology," she said. "I shouldn't have been so rude yesterday."

Charlie started to touch her arm but checked the impulse and instead ran his fingers across the few remaining strands of hair on top of his head. "I understand. Believe me, I know what you're going through. It helps to talk about the pain, although I don't do enough of that myself." To be honest, he never discussed Mamie's death, not even with their kids.

She raised her eyebrows. "You mean...you?"

"Yes. Me, too." He pursed his lips. "Mamie died almost two years ago. Twenty-two months and three weeks, to be exact. And it still hurts. I think it will always hurt."

Instantly, the old familiar despair surfaced, eager to drag him down into its cold abyss. Charlie drew a long breath and then exhaled. "I hope you won't think I'm being forward, but I'd like to talk, if you have a minute."

She surveyed the nearby booths and tables. "Looks like a good time for a short break. But I'd better get your order first."

"How about bringing us each one of Sam's giant cinnamon rolls?"

Pencil poised above her order pad, she eyed him for a moment. "I shouldn't. They're loaded with calories..." She brightened. "I hear he makes the best cinnamon rolls in town. And I keep saying I want to get back into life. What better way?" She scribbled on the pad. "Two C-rolls coming up."

When she finished, she winked at him. "So, mister, are you game for a cup of my brew?"

Charlie grinned. "That's why I'm here." He watched her

walk away. It felt good to laugh again.

———————

That afternoon, Charlie met his youngest daughter, Susan, for lunch at their favorite restaurant a block from his downtown Denver law office. After placing their orders, she leaned toward him, eyebrows scrunched. He sat back, sensing she was about to say something he might not want to hear.

"Okay, Dad. Tell me. What happened?"

"What do you mean?"

"You seem more like your old self today. You're bouncier, peppier—happier. Something's changed."

He took a sip of water. "I don't know what you're talking about." She'd always been the curious one in the family.

Susan rested both forearms on the table. "After Mom died, you left us. Oh, you were here physically, but that was all. Yet, today you're different."

"Different, huh?"

"Yeah."

"Well, I don't feel much different." He scratched his jaw.

"Aha." Her amber eyes narrowed. "So, you do feel a little bit different. Something has changed. Right, Dad?"

"I guess you could say that, but..."

She clasped her hands together. "Please, Dad, please tell me what happened."

Charlie looked at his daughter, at the pedestrians walking in the bright sunshine on the other side of the window and then back at her. "I suppose you could say something happened, but it's really nothing." He toyed with a spoon. "You'll probably think it's silly."

"No way." She flipped her blond hair behind her shoulders. "What is it? You know I'm dying of curiosity."

He laughed. "I've not doubted that since this conversation began."

"So..."

He took a breath. "Well, I met this, this lady, and—"

"Oh, Dad!" She squealed. "I should have known it. That's wonderful. I can't wait to tell Stephanie and Greg you're in love again."

Charlie held up his hand. "Susan..." He had to stop her before she did one of her signature happy dances right there in the middle of the restaurant.

"Oh, uh, sorry. I got carried away." She rested her chin on her hands. "Tell me all about her."

Charlie felt his face grow warm. "Well, actually, I, I don't know much. She's a waitress and newly widowed and, well, that's about it."

"What does she look like?"

"Mmm...medium-length hair, I think. Or short. Maybe brown." He tried to remember. "Maybe gray." He rubbed his sweaty hands against his pant legs. "She, she looks like, like a woman. That's how she looks. Not fat, not skinny—or tall or short."

"Okay... How old is she?"

"I don't know." He ran a finger through the condensation on his water glass. "About your mother's age, I suppose. Maybe younger."

The interrogation continued. "What's her name?"

"I, I haven't asked." He silently cursed the moisture

[49]

coating his armpits. Now he'd have to drop his jacket by the dry cleaners, something Mamie used to do for him.

"Ooh," Susan teased. "Some romance."

"I just met her." He folded his arms and glanced around for the waiter. Their food was taking way too long. "I need to get back to work."

She lowered her head. "Sorry. That wasn't funny." She fidgeted with her napkin. "But even if you don't know her very well, she's sparked new life in you. That's great. Are you planning to ask her out?"

Charlie's eyes widened. "I can't do that. I'm a married..."

Susan shook her head. "Not anymore. We all loved Mom, and we all miss her—a lot. But it's been almost two years, Dad. It might do you good to get out and socialize a bit."

"I'm not so sure, honey." Charlie crumpled his napkin into a ball. "Your mother was the only one I *socialized* with for thirty-seven years. I'd feel like an adulterous traitor with anyone else."

Her eyes filled with compassion. "It'll be hard." She placed her hand on top of his. "But you should ask her out." She winked. "Once you learn her name, of course."

———

Monday morning, Charlie woke long before dawn. Hands behind his head, he stretched and grinned, already thinking of the previous evening. That Amanda was something else. Been a long time since he'd had so much fun, if that was the word for talking until midnight. He yawned a long hard yawn.

But the evening wasn't all peaches and cream. When

he picked Amanda up at her house, her college-age girls had eyed him like a couple wild cats itching to tear him apart. If only he could tell them he knew far too well how much they hurt, that he'd treat their grieving mother with respect—that he wasn't trying to replace their father.

Though he tried, Charlie couldn't go back to sleep. He showered and dressed and was about to walk through the door that led to the garage, when the thought struck him. Amanda might think he was moving in on her if he showed up at the café early, especially after keeping her up so late last night.

He dropped his briefcase by the door and stomped into the kitchen to jerk a cereal box from the cupboard. "Get involved with a woman, and a man can't even eat where or when he wants anymore." Glaring at Mamie's placid picture on the countertop, he continued, "What do I do tomorrow, and the next day? It's all your fault, you know. How could you leave me in this mess? How dare you—?"

Charlie stopped his ranting, put down the box and picked up the picture. He traced the flat, lifeless outline of his wife's face with his finger. "I'm sorry," he whispered. "I know it's not your fault. And I know you don't want to hear about another woman. The truth is, it's you I want, and only you."

He clutched the picture to his chest. "I miss you, Mamie. Every minute of every day."

———

A young man waited on him Wednesday morning, and Amanda was nowhere in sight. By the time the waiter brought his order, Charlie could no longer constrain himself. With forced casualness, he said, "I thought

Amanda Wilson worked this shift. Does she have the day off?"

"I think that's the lady I replaced." The waiter poured him another cup of coffee. "As far as I know, she doesn't work here anymore."

"I see." Charlie felt a dull thud in his stomach. "Just curious."

His appetite gone, Charlie rolled the newspaper and trudged toward his office. It was his fault. Amanda's girls didn't like him—and maybe she felt the same way, but she didn't know how to tell him, so she quit her job.

The instant he settled behind his desk, Charlie reached for the telephone, determined to call Amanda and apologize. She had kids in college. She needed that job. But each time he lifted the receiver, his courage vanished.

After what felt like hours of pacing and mumbling in front of the window between attempts to write a complicated divorce agreement, Charlie checked his watch. Ridiculous. He hadn't gotten a thing done all day.

He kicked his chair under the desk and punched the intercom button. At the sound of his secretary's voice, he bellowed, "Cancel me out for the afternoon. *All* my appointments. I'm going fishing."

———————

When the westward-bound freeway finally escaped the suburbs, Charlie rolled down his window and sucked in a deep gulp of fresh spring air. "Ah, this is more like it. That blasted smog is gonna kill me yet."

He turned off the radio and relaxed in his seat, relishing the sight of the majestic Rocky Mountains that towered ahead of him. Had to be months, maybe years since he'd been fishing. Come to think of it, he hadn't been to the fishing hole since Mamie died, even though he renewed his fishing license every year. Before he could succumb to the pain again, he pounded the dashboard. "I'm gonna enjoy this!"

A glance at the empty passenger seat, however, filled him with another kind of sorrow. Mamie wasn't the only one he missed. He missed his dad, too. They'd had some good times fishing together, some real good times. Unbelievable the way that man could find fish. They always came home with a catch.

Soon, he was rattling across the isolated dirt road that led to his father's favorite fishing hole. The access was rockier than ever, which was okay if it kept people out. But when he neared the creek, he saw the reflection of light off metal and groaned. Someone had found their spot.

Charlie parked behind the lone four-wheel-drive pickup, muttering, "Of all the luck. I was hoping for a little peace and quiet." He debated whether or not to turn around and go back to town but finally got out of the car. He'd come all this way. Might as well fish for a bit.

Opening the trunk where he'd kept his tackle box and pole for more years than he could remember, he realized he was still wearing his jacket. If he was going to keep doing this, he'd have to put some old clothes in the car. Mamie would have skinned his hide for mucking around in a suit.

Charlie set the equipment beside the car and closed the trunk lid. He took off his jacket and tie, tossed them onto the front seat, rolled up his sleeves and grabbed his gear. Before he began the descent to the creek, which ran parallel with the road but lower on the hillside, he breathed in the fresh, clean, pine scent and scanned the creek bank, pleased the area hadn't changed much. Evergreen branches highlighted the white trunks and chartreuse leaves on the spring-awakened aspen trees. Sunshine reflected off rippling water, and a kaleidoscope of wildflowers blanketed the clearing on the opposite hillside.

He worked his way down the incline, alternately sliding on the slick soles of his dress shoes and digging in his heels. Near the bottom, where the surging mountain stream formed a pool, Charlie stopped to catch his breath. He peered through the foliage, thinking he'd find a spot as far as possible from the other fisherman—or fisherwoman. What were they s'posed to call people these days, anyway? Fisherperson?

A young male voice called, "Come on down. The fish are biting."

With a grunt and a groan, he finished the descent and settled onto a large rock that jutted out from the grassy shelf. He nodded at the thin young man several feet from him. "So the fish are biting, huh? What're you catching?"

The other man grinned. "Rainbows!" He held up a string of three. "Aren't these beauties?"

"Sure are." The guy was friendly enough. But Charlie didn't know what to think about the beard—or the grungy clothing. Maybe he was homeless. Probably had to fish to eat.

Eyeing Charlie's white shirt and dress pants, the other man said, "Looks like you took off in a hurry. Did you get lunch?"

Charlie shook his head and offered a sheepish grin. "Guess I was anxious to get out of the office." He unfastened the top button of his shirt. "Hadn't even realized it was lunch time."

"I'm just finishing my lunch. I'd be glad to share the leftovers. My wife fixed enough for a Boy Scout troop."

"I could use a bite, if you're sure you can spare it."

The fisherman scooted close and reached out a hand. "Bob Mason."

"Charlie." He shook the younger man's hand. "Charlie Burns."

"Nice to meet you, Charlie." Bob turned to dig through his cooler. "How does a tuna sandwich on wholegrain bread and some carrot sticks sound?"

"Delicious—and a lot better for my cholesterol levels than what I've been eating lately."

The two fished without speaking until Charlie felt a powerful tug on his line. "Hey," he said, "feels like I've got a whopper. This is still the best fishing hole around."

"Oops." Bob grimaced. "I horned in on your territory."

Charlie didn't respond until he landed the trout. "I've been fishing this pond for forty years, but I don't own it—although my dad might have argued that point, if he were still around."

Bob laughed. "I discovered it a few weeks ago, the first time my wife kicked me out of the store."

Charlie gave him a questioning glance and laid the fish on the rock.

"It's not as bad as it sounds. We bought a health food store in Evergreen a while back, and we're just getting it off the ground. If I spend too much time with the books, my mind starts to explode. That's the way it feels, anyway. So, Barb tells me I have to go fishing one afternoon a week. Some dame, huh?"

"Sounds like you reeled in a beauty." Charlie smiled. "I'd say she's a keeper."

"She is." Bob attached a new fly to his line. "I almost blew it after our third date, though. I called and called her apartment, but she never answered. And every time I tried to get her at the place where she worked, they just said, 'She's out, and we don't know when she'll return.'

"Same words every time, like a recording. Drove me nuts. I finally decided she was avoiding me and stopped calling.

"But I couldn't stop thinking about her. So I drove by her apartment one night. Took me forever to work up the nerve, but I eventually got out of the car and knocked on her door. Someone else answered. When I asked for Barb, the woman said, 'She's in the hospital. I'm just here to feed her cat.' I said, 'What?' and found out she'd been in a bad car wreck.

"I rushed straight from there to the hospital, breaking the speed limit all the way. And..." He shrugged his shoulders. "Things went from there."

Charlie grinned. "That's what I like to hear. Happy endings."

Bob tossed his line across the water again. "One more round, and I'd better head back to start dinner. Doesn't seem right to make my wife run the store alone and cook, too. Besides, she loves the way I fix trout."

Honeybees buzzed in the wild strawberry bushes that surrounded Charlie's rock, zipping from one blossom to the next. In the tree branches above, birds chirped a happy serenade to springtime. Water gurgled and splashed at his feet, and sunshine saturated his winter-weary bones.

Charlie caught one more fish, moved to the shade and fell asleep in the grass. When he awoke, the air had cooled and the shadows of the pines stretched across the creek. He brushed off his clothing and gathered his things to climb the rocky hill to his car.

Before he stashed his gear, he drew one last gulp of mountain air. His dad was right. Best medicine in the world.

The sun was almost down when he pulled into his garage. Charlie lifted the bucket of fish from the trunk, slammed it shut and strode whistling into the kitchen. Thanks to Bob's generosity, he had more fish than he could possibly eat. Maybe he'd give his secretary a couple.

After emptying the trout into the sink, he kissed Mamie's picture. "Guess who I ran into at the convenience store down the street." He chuckled. "You'll never guess. I was so surprised I could barely speak."

Seeing his wife's face reminded Charlie how she hated it when he tracked dirt into the house. He returned to the garage to clean the dried mud off his shoes and pant legs and retrieve his clothing from the front seat of his car.

Back in the kitchen, which now smelled like fish, he continued his monologue. "Amanda's oldest daughter. That's who I saw. She actually acted happy to see me." Shaking his head, he pulled out a stool to sit at the counter. "Wonders never cease." He cocked his head. "Maybe I read her and her sister wrong. Anyway, when I asked how her mom was doing, she told me a family friend offered her a job with better pay and a shorter commute."

One elbow on the counter, Charlie leaned close to blow dust off the picture. His neighbor lady cleaned house for him, but she and her husband were on an extended vacation. "Although I wasn't too happy to hear she was no longer at the café, I said, 'Please congratulate Amanda for me.'"

He moved the portrait next to the empty fruit bowl but then decided it looked better on the corner and set it there. "She got this funny expression on her face, said her mom missed me and she was hoping I'd call her again. I must have looked as surprised as I felt because she laughed. 'Mom is, like, way old-fashioned.' He mimicked the girl's high voice and disgusted expression. 'She thinks men are s'posed to call women, not the other way around.' Then she did that eye-rolling thing our daughters used to do."

Reliving the awkward encounter made Charlie feel warm all over. He ran the back of his hand across his forehead. "Once again, I was at a loss for words. You know how I stutter and stammer when I'm in a jam. Eventually, I managed to tell her I'd call her mom—soon."

He reached for the telephone. "Now is as good a time as any."

With a grin and a wink, he added, "You know what I think, babe? I think a fish fry would be a great way for our kids to get to know Amanda and her girls."

THE HAND OF THE PRINCESS

Lisa Michelle Hess

Gather your rags around you, children, and come sit close. Quiet now, and I'll tell you a story. I know, little one. Just try to cough softly.

This is a story about two boys and a girl not much older than some of you in the time before this time, when the world still seemed sane. It was before The Wars, when there was electricity twenty-four hours a day and most people, not just the government, had a computer. What I'm about to tell you happened in a peaceful little town not far from here. The hero of this story was named Arturo, and he was in love with a girl named Gwen, and she was in love with him.

Back in those days, children didn't talk to each other face-to-face the way you do now. They lived their lives in a virtual computer world, where they would tell all the inhabitants their thoughts, dreams, desires and fantasies by writing on their virtual walls, which were something like public billboards. They would fall in love, fight, break up, and get back together—all for everyone in their virtual worlds to see. They would display pictures of themselves, hundreds of them, doing all kinds of things. Making faces, laughing with friends, standing in line at a theater. They called hanging their lives on the walls of this world "posting."

Much of what they posted included information you children would think of as private, things to be hidden and only whispered about to your closest friends, so that strangers would not know who or where you were and, therefore, could not find you and hurt you.

But the world was different then. These children perceived no danger. Indeed, they felt safer in their virtual world than they did in the real world. Gwen could be sitting right next to her best friend, Megan, but if she had something to say to her, she would write it and post it to her friend's virtual wall. That way, the people who lived in the real world wouldn't hear them.

They thought their secrets were safe, until the night everything changed...but, I'm getting ahead of myself.

It all started when Gwen had her nails done. In those days, children also published their stories on their bodies. Their hair—colors of pink and purple, magenta and black—reflected their moods. Their bodies were covered with permanent pictures and words that recorded the history of their lives, adventures and loves. Even their nails were bejeweled and painted with perfect, intricate designs.

On this particular day, Gwen thought her nails were so fantastically done and so pretty, she couldn't wait to show all her friends. So, of course, she took a self-portrait with her phone camera. The black-and-white photo showed her spread fingers tipped with perfect nails completely obscuring her face, except for one beautiful, dark, dramatically lined eye, and her tousled hair spilling over her forehead. She posted the picture to her virtual wall. Never having been shy, Gwen titled the photo *The Hand of the Princess.*

The picture was a sensation. All her friends loved it. Within hours, twenty comments were posted saying how gorgeous Gwen looked, how wonderful her nails turned out, and how the viewers couldn't stop looking at the picture.

When Gwen's friends commented on her picture, the comment and the picture appeared on their virtual walls. Then their friends commented on the photo. And so it went. The comments piled up, page after page, and became increasingly more sophisticated.

Some mentioned Gwen's mature use of perspective, contrast and lighting. Others asked about her artistic influences and wanted to know which galleries featured her work. For a while, Gwen was famous because of that picture, and everyone in her small town knew about it.

One of the comments caused quite a stir. It came from Gwen's ex-boyfriend, Lance, who'd moved to the city the year before. The comment wasn't long. It simply read: *Wow! When did you get so hot?*

Within minutes, Arturo posted a follow-up comment. *Dude, she's always been hot. And quit talking about her like she's yours when she's not.*

Now, you must understand that Arturo and Lance had been friends since they were small children, even though they were from two different...tribes, you might say, which had little in common. Their friendship began in preschool. One day when their mothers arrived to pick them up from daycare, a place where children stayed and played while their mothers worked, Arturo and Lance were wrestling.

In fact, they'd been wrestling and fighting all day, and their teacher was only too glad to see their mothers. The two outraged boys, who looked almost like brothers but not quite, were locked in mortal combat. The mothers quickly sized up the situation and pulled them apart, while the boys continued to hurl insults at each other.

Arturo yelled, "You're a silly little *chica* running to your mama."

Lance had no idea what *chica* meant, but he knew it wasn't good. He thought fast, trying to come up with something just as bad to fling back at the other boy. A word popped into his head he *thought* he'd heard an older boy in his tribe use to describe a farm worker. "Oh, yeah?" Lance clamped his tiny hands on his little hips and pooched out his bottom lip. "Well, you're just a bean." When he didn't receive the response he was hoping for, he realized he hadn't repeated the insult quite right.

Arturo was puzzled and had no idea why being a "bean" would be bad. He liked beans. But his mother had gasped, so he shouted the only thing he could think of back at Lance. "Oh, yeah, well...well...you're just a red bean!"

Fists clenched, both boys stared at each other as stillness enveloped the room. Then the boys' teacher and their mothers dissolved into chuckles that turned into peals of laughter, which only got louder the longer the hilarity lasted and ended with tears streaming down the women's faces.

The boys shrugged. Their mothers appeared to be friends and seemed to be having a great time together. So they figured they could be friends, too. And they were, from that time forward. Until they met Gwen.

Gwen moved to town when she was fifteen and the boys a year older. Auburn-haired, with light, light skin and eyes so dark they were almost black, she was just beginning to grow into the striking woman she would become. A city girl with wild clothes and a ring in her nose, she exuded a confidence unmatched by the small-town girls the boys had known all their lives.

For an entire year, they avoided her, feeling outclassed by her sophisticated ways. But eventually, she let them into her virtual world—called "friending," and they, along with all the other children in town, soon inhabited the same virtual universe.

Before long, Lance, the more assertive of the two, began to flirt with Gwen. He praised her virtual photo album, commented when her pictures showed she'd changed her hair or had a new tattoo—and then, he actually started calling her on the phone.

The other girls in town tried to warn Gwen.

Lance would post, *You're my greatest fantasy.*

Tayla would add, *I remember when you used to say that to me.*

Or Lance would comment, *I took a long drive and thought about you all the way.*

Emily would respond, *Hey! You said you were thinking about me yesterday.*

Lance was glib, confident and funny. He had lots of friends and relatives he posted with in the city. His writing was bold and edgy, something Gwen missed from her city days.

Just before the boys graduated from high school, Lance and Gwen began spending time together in the real world. But their romance didn't last. Gwen felt awkward around Lance. He was too good-looking, too self-assured, and it wasn't long before she realized the other girls were right. He was a player who didn't have time for anyone's dreams but his own.

Arturo watched all this from afar. He knew Lance, and he knew he would soon tire of this latest girl. Arturo was polite to Gwen, but he didn't treat her like she was anything special. She was the only woman in the world he'd ever really wanted, but Lance was his best friend. So he hid his feelings, and waited.

And it seemed Arturo's plan worked. Lance commented less and less on Gwen's postings and pictures. When his comments did appear, they were patronizing and tinged with sarcasm. Eventually, Lance stopped calling. On top of that, he unfriended Gwen, which was their generation's ultimate rejection.

Lance and Gwen didn't actually break up, because they hadn't been officially "together." And Gwen had begun to distance herself from Lance. But, still, his unfriending hurt. As you might guess, Arturo was there to pick up the pieces.

What neither Gwen nor Arturo perceived was that Lance wasn't as blind as they'd thought. He *had* started to fall for Gwen. This girl, unlike any other, was the one person who could get in the way of all his dreams, the one who could keep him in that small town. So he cut her loose, before she tied him down.

After he left, Lance and Gwen revived their virtual relationship. He friended her, and she friended him. It was all very friendly. Until Lance saw her *Hand of the Princess* portrait. Surprised by the feeling of loss he experienced, he'd posted the comment about Gwen.

And then Arturo and Lance weren't friends anymore.

It was a short time later that Gwen's brother became very ill. The problem wasn't as dire as it seemed. The medical community had a procedure to fix the problem. But the challenge was, of course, money. Gwen's family didn't have the funds to pay for the procedure.

One night, while Gwen lay listening to her brother's tortured breathing in the next room, she hit upon a plan. She threw off her covers and flipped open her computer. After a moment, she typed this: *For my brother who's sick and in great distress, I'm auctioning off The Hand of the Princess. One large copy is signed and completed. All other copies will be deleted!*

She took a deep breath and pushed the post button.

The world being what it was, most people had forgotten about Gwen and her picture and moved on to the next latest sensation. But in that small town, both the girl and the picture were still famous. When she announced that a poster-sized portrait would be auctioned off in a week at the local Players Theatre, the posts began to fly.

Lance wrote: *That picture will be mine. I'll arrive the night before. Seeing you would be fine. I'll be knocking at your door.*

Innocently, Gwen responded: *I've missed you, my friend. I'll take what help I can get. Who'll end up with the picture? It's anyone's bet.*

Arturo wrote: *You know, this really isn't a competition. We're helping Gwen's brother. It's about his condition.*

The back-and-forth posts went on for days.

Arturo tried not to be jealous. He trusted Gwen, and truth be told, he still had a soft spot for his longtime buddy, Lance. But he knew how charming Lance could be, and he knew Gwen had once been attracted to him. Although he didn't want to play the jealous lover, Arturo couldn't help but ask Gwen in a post what she would do if Lance really did show up at her door.

Her response was simple. *This is something you'll have to rise above. Chemistry happens, but that's not love.*

Her answer didn't help Arturo feel better. He knew Lance had received a substantial amount of money from a trust fund on his eighteenth birthday. He'd purchased a convertible and cool clothes, set aside enough money for college, and still had loads of cash left over.

On the other hand, Arturo was barely making ends meet as an assistant manager at the local grocery store. He still lived with his parents and drove the beater he'd had all through high school. He thought about Gwen choosing between him and Lance the night of the auction, and he imagined the choice wouldn't be very hard.

As tormented as he was by his thoughts of Lance and Gwen, Arturo was equally tortured by the pain her brother endured. Arturo didn't just love Gwen, he loved her entire family. He thought of her brother as his little brother, too. He sincerely wanted to do something to ease his pain, but what?

The night before the auction, Lance made a grand appearance at Gwen's door, all charm and swagger. He swept her into his arms and gave her a hug that lifted her off her feet. She shrieked, hugged him back, and then laughingly told him to put her down.

She ushered him into her house to see the rest of the family, but before she shut the door, she scanned up and down the street. No Arturo. She hadn't seen or heard from him in three days. Surely he'd come to see his friend. But Arturo stayed away.

All evening, Lance and Gwen sat in her kitchen, catching up and laughing about how silly they'd been when they were young. Her brother joined them for a time but tired quickly. Gwen watched him as he slowly made his way up the stairs to his bedroom, and Lance saw the boy's pain reflected in Gwen's anxious eyes. In that instant, what Arturo had been trying to tell him in his posts became real to Lance. This wasn't a game—it was life or death. Sitting next to the woman he may or may not have loved, Lance's view of his world began to change.

He wanted to tell Gwen it would be okay, that somehow he would help her brother. All the way to her house, he'd been consumed with a fantasy that began when he kissed her full lips and felt her melt in his arms. Now, all he wanted was to smooth away the worry lines around her pretty mouth and see her lips curve into the carefree, confident smile he remembered.

But he couldn't do any of those things.

He could have posted his feelings, but he didn't know how to say them out loud, and he couldn't make her brother better. So he said the only thing he could manage. "Gwen, I'm so sorry." He pulled her into a hug and vowed to help her, somehow.

She searched his eyes, smiled and pushed him away. She was going to bed, she said. If he really wanted to help, he should bid up the picture the following night.

Lance showed himself out.

That night, one lonely post appeared on Arturo's wall. *Where are you, Arturo? I miss you so.*

The night of the auction, the entire town descended on the Players Theatre. Some were there to bid, some to watch the bidding. Many, it was said, had come to see the showdown that was sure to happen between Lance and Arturo. But those people were sadly disappointed because Arturo wasn't there.

Gwen worked her way through the crowd dressed like an on-trend princess in a blue-velvet and silver-satin empire-waist sheath. She kept a smile plastered on her face, waved to friends in the balcony and thanked as many people as possible for coming, always with one eye on the door.

Finally, when it seemed everyone who was coming must have arrived, Gwen unveiled the portrait on the stage to gasps of admiration and applause from the crowd. The auction began and, still, no Arturo.

Bidding started at three-hundred dollars but moved up fast. In minutes, people were bidding five hundred, a thousand, then five thousand—and they didn't stop there. As the bidding inched its way toward ten-thousand dollars, it seemed many times each bid would be the final one, only to be topped at the last minute, to the delighted applause of the crowd.

By the time the bids reached ten thousand, there were only a few bidders left. Lance was one of them, which would have left Gwen with mixed feelings, if she'd had time to think about it. But her thoughts were entirely occupied with hope for her brother and apprehension about Arturo's absence. She feared something dire must have happened to him.

Lance was thinking about Gwen and what he'd discovered earlier in the day regarding costs for her brother's treatment. Though the bidding had climbed past fifteen-thousand dollars, the sum wasn't even half of what was needed. As the sun set behind the theater and the bidding continued to rise, he also knew he might very well be throwing away his entire inheritance for a woman who loved someone else.

The bidding was slowing down. The local bank CEO had finally thrown in the towel, and the only two bidders left were Lance and an art collector from out of town. Of course, the town was rooting for Lance to win over the outsider.

The bidding inched up, fifteen-one, fifteen-two. The collector matched Lance, bid for bid, sixteen thousand, sixteen-five. Lance made eye-contact with Gwen, who was across the room. She shook her head, a gesture he knew meant this was her burden, not his. Then she turned with another worried, longing look toward the empty theater entrance.

Lance clenched his fists and felt the anger like a liquid boiling in his chest. He wished for a wall to punch, but the crowd surrounded him on every side. He couldn't stand to see Gwen hurting, and he was mad at Arturo for causing her pain. Yet, it was more than that. He hated the whole tangled mess and, most of all, he missed the best friend he'd ever had. The thought washed over him like a revelation. He loved them both in a rare way. Theirs was a friendship that transcended lust or greed or rivalry—and he would do anything to preserve it.

The auctioneer was saying it again: "Going once...going twice."

Lance held up his paddle and bid his entire future. "Twenty-five thousand dollars." His voice was strong and sure.

The crowd gasped and jumped to their feet.

"Going once...going twice...SOLD to the young man in the front row." There was an explosion of whistles, shouts and applause. People surrounded Lance, congratulating him, patting him on the back. He lost sight of Gwen and then saw her on the other side of the theater talking to Megan.

Smiling at the people he'd grown up with, thanking them for coming, saying it was the least he could do, he worked his way slowly through the crowd to Megan and Gwen. He must have looked like he always did, swaggering and self-assured. But he didn't feel it.

The girls had their heads close together. Megan thrust a piece of paper into Gwen's hands and whispered urgently in her ear. At first, Gwen looked mystified, but then tears started to run down her face, too many to wipe away.

All the onlookers saw was Gwen staring at a piece of paper and crying and Lance looking over her shoulder at it with a perplexed expression that quickly changed to resignation. Some said in that instant he looked older, while the more perceptive of them used words like "weary" and "wise."

At that point, the collector who'd been bidding against Lance placed a hand on his shoulder. The two men talked for a minute. Lance looked at Gwen, who smiled up at him and nodded. Lance and the collector shook hands. The man walked away, and Lance turned to whisper in Gwen's ear. She hugged him, and then, hand-in-hand, the pair hurried toward the exit.

That was the last most people in that small town ever saw of Arturo, Lance and Gwen. Most figured Arturo knew he was beat and that Lance and Gwen had run off together. Yet, there was enough money for all the medical treatment Gwen's brother needed to make a full recovery, and he did.

Along with Megan, he kept the whereabouts of the three friends secret for many months. But, finally, Megan broke the silence with this post: *Arturo did what he thought was right. He joined the war, and so much more. The front is a nightmare, our men are in flight, and they'll pay a king's ransom for a boy to fight.*

Arturo had tired of middle management. Plus, he'd lost Gwen. Why not join the army and save her brother in the process? That was the message he'd sent with Megan to Gwen that night, along with the check the government gave him to enlist and a life insurance policy with Gwen as the sole beneficiary.

Did Lance end up with Gwen, after all? Patience, child. My story isn't finished.

When Lance and Gwen left the theater, they climbed into Lance's car, drove all night, and made it to the army base at dawn the next morning, just as Arturo was climbing onto a bus that would carry him far, far away.

He heard someone call his name and turned to see Gwen running toward him. Behind her, he saw Lance leaning casually against the fender of his car. Arturo shrugged. It was all right. He'd known Gwen would end up with his childhood friend.

But then he saw Gwen's face. He could see she'd been crying. Her eyes were red and her make-up smeared. Barefoot and wearing a beautiful crumpled dress he hadn't seen before, she looked like a ravished princess.

What had Lance done to her?

Before Arturo could move or say a word, Gwen threw herself into his arms and clung to him as if she'd never let go.

Stunned, he pulled back and held her at arm's length.

She smiled the old Gwen smile, confident and fond, with just a hint of amusement, and punched him, not gently, in the shoulder. Then she kissed him and said, "Oh, Arturo, don't even start. Lance won my hand, but you own my heart."

He promised he would come back for her, and she promised she would wait forever.

What happened after that? Well, Lance sold the photo, with Gwen's blessing, to the art collector and recouped most of the cost. He returned to college, but it wasn't long before every young man of fighting age was drafted. Last I heard, Lance and Arturo ended up in the same unit. How that story unwinds is yet to be written.

And Gwen? Many people say she went to art school, which she did, in a way. I have it on good authority she did what she'd always wanted to do. She attended beauty school.

Let me see that hand, little one. I think I might be able to do something about those nails...tomorrow. Right now, children, it's off to bed with you.

Now, now, none of that. There are many more stories and nights enough to tell you all of them while we wait down here for this current wind to blow over. I'll tell you another good story tomorrow, although *The Hand of the Princess,* I must admit, has always been my favorite.

———————

CHAPEL OF THE SACRED BRAMBLE

Peter Leavell

Judas gripped the dagger hilt and slid around the corner, his back against the shadowed building. Tonight, while moon shone brightly enough to light his way, he would flee the monastery. He had to go. If he didn't leave now, he'd be no different than the other monks whose souls and bodies shriveled like dates under the merciless desert sun. In time, even their intellects succumbed to the isolation and the hot winds that blasted sand into every crevice of every building, bed and body.

The monks' destiny was no secret. The desert drove them to insanity.

Rather than lose his mind in the midst of dry winds and equally dry brothers, he would gain the world. Soon, all Byzantium would know the name *Judas the Monk*. Jesus' fallen disciple would be remembered no more, and the name Judas would become synonymous with *healing*, *hope* and *generosity*, rather than greed and betrayal.

Like a wary desert leopard, the monastery crouched halfway up Mount Sinai's rocky slope. Judas eyed the rugged peak and wondered if those who built the hermitage thought they would somehow protect Moses' sacred encounters with Jehovah. The full moon hovered just above the barren mountain, casting a silver glow against the monastery wall and the noiseless structures contained within.

He pulled the hood of his wool robe over his head, the smell of stale cloth filling his nostrils. He concealed the knife deep within the wide sleeves and listened for activity. Hearing nothing, he stepped onto the worn stone path that ran between the buildings.

A moist, clean smell drifted on the wind, the first he'd encountered in months. Perhaps it had rained somewhere. Perhaps he would find that place soon. An owl called into the night, the only sound other than the shuffle of his sandals and palm branches rattling in the breeze.

He passed the cells where the other monks slept. He knew they were desperate for rest before midnight prayers—the latest intolerable creation of the abbot. Empty black windows seemed to stare back at him. He hurried on.

Judas followed the path to the Chapel of the Sacred Bramble. Outside the small sanctuary, a warm wind rustled the sacrosanct bush. As he'd done hundreds of times before, he tried to envision himself in Moses' sandals, watching the fire of God burn, yet seeing the shrub remain whole and unscathed. But he couldn't recreate the hallowed moment.

Since he'd arrived at the monastery, he'd witnessed only one miracle. That event had occurred inside the chapel. With a shaking hand, he opened the heavy wooden door, slipped inside and closed it without a sound.

Their order's tradition maintained that a lamp was to burn in the chapel at all times. But, lately, olive oil had been scarce. Darkness smothered the tiny, airless room.

Judas blinked as he turned, and then blinked again. The desert held such incredible absence of light, but this was the last time he would have to endure its blinding shroud. He took eight steps forward, imagining the vacant wooden benches on either side of the center aisle, and stopped when he neared the front. The only sound was his heavy breathing.

He sucked in a whiff of sand-scented dust and covered his nostrils with his sleeve. Turning to the left, he took three paces, reached out and wrapped his fingers around a wooden icon he knew stood no taller than his forearm. The Virgin Mary.

Three days ago, Mary had cried. He'd seen her tears during his prayers and later told the abbot. But he'd been rebuffed. The abbot said he believed him but insisted he not tell the others. It was not their place to know.

He'd mulled the abbot's words for two days. Finally, he understood why his superior failed to comprehend the icon's potential. The desert had driven him mad. That's when Judas decided to take Mary to Constantinople, where all would see the wonders of her powers.

With care, he extended the knife, slipped the blade under the base and dislodged the statue from the pedestal.

The door behind him opened.

Judas dropped the statue and spun around. Shadows danced with candlelight in the doorway. He rolled under a bench, praying he hadn't been seen or heard, and watched a hooded monk shuffle down the aisle, holding a candle in front of him.

When the monk reached the front of the sanctuary, he whispered, "Dear God..." and set the candle on the bench above Judas. Kneeling beside the Virgin's toppled form, he picked her up and carefully dusted her with his sleeve. Then he ran a finger over her cheeks, as if wiping away tears.

Judas frowned. This monk, a kindly man he'd served and worshiped with for years, knew the Virgin's secret—and he was obviously about to steal her.

Judas scrambled to his feet and snatched the icon from the other man's hands.

The monk screeched, "No!" and leapt at Judas, grasping the statue with both hands.

Before his fellow cleric could gain the advantage, Judas drove the dagger deep into his chest. A gagging sound erupted from the man's throat as both men slipped to the ground. Judas rolled away from the dead monk, lifted the candle from the bench and set it in the icon's nook. A sticky wetness covered his hand. He wiped it on the fallen monk's robe.

Footsteps echoed outside.

Judas wrenched the knife from the monk's chest and stood. He'd killed for the Virgin. He would do it again.

The abbot and Brother Simeon stepped into the doorway. The candles they held illuminated their faces. They stared at him and then moved in unison toward the front.

Judas looked down and saw the knife in one of his hands, the icon in the other. Blood stained both of their robes. He glanced again at Mary's face. She was watching him with large, swollen eyes. Human eyes filled with life. His hands shook, and so did she.

The voice of the abbot penetrated his growing fear. "What happened, Brother Judas? Was Brother John stealing the statue?"

Still staring at the statue, Judas nodded. The accusing eyes penetrated his soul, slashing it in two. He felt as dead as the man at his feet, yet his heart surged in his chest.

He flung the icon against the wall. The wooden figure bounced onto the stone floor and spun in a circle. Still, the Virgin's reproving gaze remained locked on him.

Judas dropped the knife and shoved past the abbot and Brother Simeon. Sprinting as fast as his robe and sandals allowed, he ran along the monastery walls, past gardens, cells and workrooms to clatter down a narrow flight of steps. He had to escape the desert before it drove him crazy.

Halfway down the stairs, he tripped and fell to the bottom. A wicked crack reverberated through his skull. He tried to get up, but his limbs didn't respond, and his head was twisted at a horrible angle on the warm stone. Why couldn't he breathe? Why couldn't he move?

The abbot and Brother Simeon knelt beside him. Clutched in the abbot's hand, Mary turned her face away from Judas.

Black shadows narrowed his vision. He heard Simeon say, "But I saw her gaze, Father."

"It was not meant for you."

Though Judas struggled for a breath, his lungs refused

to draw in air.

"Quiet." The abbot held up a hand. "She speaks." He lifted the icon to his ear.

Judas heard a faint whisper. Did the abbot's lips move? He didn't think so.

Simeon asked, "What did she say?"

The abbot sighed. "It seems the desert has driven our dear Brother Judas insane."

————————

FOLLOW THE MOONBEAM

Rebecca Carey Lyles

Marie unlatched the screen door and was about to step out, when Dan said, "Back at it?" She turned, surprised she'd heard his voice over the sound of the ballgame on the television.

Dan was seated in his recliner, an open newspaper in his hands and an odd expression on his face. "Snooping on the twins again?"

Since when did her husband of twenty-seven years look away from a game long enough to know where she was or what she was doing? "It's research. Got a deadline." She peered through the screen at the stripe of moonlight that flowed up the steps and over their front porch. The night was bright, too bright. The kids might see her. Yet, with a deadline looming before her like Mount Everest, she had no choice.

Slipping out the door, she tiptoed toward the wooden swing, which hung in the farthest corner of the verandah.

Camouflaged by leaf shadows cast through the tall cottonwoods that lined the street, the swing was a perfect cover for her nightly observations. Marie settled onto the swing. Dan probably thought she was a pervert. And Jim and Sally would call the cops if they had any inkling she spied on their teenagers every night. But she didn't know what else to do. For the first time in her career, she was experiencing writers block.

She rubbed at the knotted muscle between her eyebrows. She'd written dozens of love stories for women's magazines plus six romance novels. Number seven shouldn't be a big deal. However, despite her initial vision for the story and her enthusiastic proposal to the publisher, this book had become a *huge* deal. Her editor expected a completed manuscript in two weeks, yet she'd only written forty-seven pages. In all her years of freelancing, she'd never missed a deadline or been at such a loss for words.

A big black cat chased a smaller striped one through the grass, hissing and growling, which caught the attention of Corky, the next-door neighbor's dog. The old Doberman hurled himself into the rickety wooden fence, wheezing a hoarse warning to the intruders. Marie scrunched low in the swing. The fence held, but Corky continued to bark long after the cats disappeared. Finally, the dog snuffled away and Marie sat up.

Sliding a pencil and a penlight from her shorts' pocket, she opened her notebook and prepared to write. She thought about the story awaiting her words. The *who, what, where, when* and *how* had come to her without a struggle, but the *why* eluded her. Love, she'd discovered, was not a romantic gondola glide down a tranquil river of bliss. Rather, it was a stomach-churning rollercoaster ride.

She tapped the pencil on her knee. Why in the world did humans strap their hearts into bone-jarring emotional roller coasters? Were the fleeting, gravity-defying highs really worth the gut-wrenching, painful descents? Was a glimpse of heaven worth the plunge into the pit of despair? Marie shook her head and turned to a new page. Goodness, she was cynical tonight. She peeked through the trees at the house across the street.

The twin girls who lived in the two-story home with their parents had recently discovered the opposite sex. Almost every evening, they sat on the front porch with their boyfriends and their dog, Squeegee. Marie smiled. Tonight, she had the light of a full moon to study their antics.

One of the girls jumped off the porch steps and skipped away, her dog and her boyfriend at her heels. Squeegee yapped and ran figure-eights around the couple. The pair on the porch laughed. The boy shouted, "Get 'em, Squeegee!"

Marie grinned but didn't feel the scene was one she could use in her novel. She glanced through the living room window. As usual, Dan had fallen asleep in his chair. The newspaper was spread on his chest like a collapsed tent, and his snores rose above the blare of the television. The remains of his warmed-up supper sat on the end table. She sighed, remembering the endless, amorous summer nights of early marriage.

She turned around in time to see the young man "capture" his partner and lead her toward a broad tree, his arm around her shoulders. Bathed in brilliant moonlight, they made a pretty picture with the dog trotting beside them. But still, Marie didn't write in her notebook. She wasn't as much interested in the touchy-feely stuff as she was in the kids' lighthearted relationships.

A cricket chirped under the porch. The moon climbed the night sky. *Heavy.* She whispered the word to the trees. Her relationship with Dan had grown so heavy. They never teased or played any more. In fact, they rarely even talked.

She leaned her head on the cushioned back of the swing, smelling the roses that bloomed beside the porch. They'd had so many good years together. When did they, how did they lose touch with each other?

Their big old house harbored happy memories of laughing, romping, door-slamming children, of frolicking puppies and frisky kittens, of neighborhood parties, holiday feasts, intimate conversations beside the fireplace—and slow dancing in the den after the children were tucked in for the night.

Maybe it was when Dan got the promotion at the refinery. From that point on, it seemed he rarely ate meals or went on outings with the family. And the pattern didn't change when their last child left home three years ago. Dan still worked long hours six, sometimes seven days a week and was usually too tired to go to a movie or out dancing on the weekends.

True, they occasionally ate lunch at a restaurant after the Sunday service, when Dan wasn't working. But they just stared at the other patrons with very little to say to each other. Was there another woman? The thought crossed her mind for the millionth time. She squeezed her eyes shut. *Don't go there, Marie.*

A girlish giggle filtered from the teenagers' direction. Marie squinted through the leaves but saw only the couple on the front steps. They appeared to be in the midst of a deep discussion. Then she noticed the leaves on the tree were rustling and shimmering in the moonlight. *Oh, my goodness, they climbed the tree. Now, there's a fun idea.* She switched on her penlight and scribbled frantically.

When she finished, she flipped off the light and sat back. What would she do with that juicy tidbit? It didn't work with the book's storyline, and she didn't have time to make major changes. She frowned and closed her notebook.

Why did she do this to herself? Romance novels weren't exactly literary works of art. Though her daughters read her stories, her husband hadn't read a single word she'd written, even though she attended every one of his company's boring award banquets.

She yawned. Most men didn't read romance novels. She understood that. But it would help if he showed a little interest in her writing. With a shove of her foot, Marie rocked the swing back and forth and watched heat lightning flash in the distance. Cool evening breezes mingled with the sultry warmth of the day, caressing her arms. A pair of fireflies flittered nearby.

Oh, Dan. You're my husband. I miss you. She looked inside. His chair was empty. He'd gone to bed without saying "goodnight," and she'd been too caught up in the neighbor kids' activities to notice when he turned off the television.

The girl on the porch leaned on her boyfriend's shoulder, apparently mesmerized by his monologue. Marie sighed. To be honest, this thing with Dan wasn't all one-sided. She didn't exactly dote on her husband these days. When the kids were still at home, she'd fixed him sack lunches for work and wrote silly love notes on the napkins. Now, he grabbed hamburgers and onion rings at the burger joint near his office, which wasn't helping his waistline—or his cholesterol levels.

She ran her fingers through her hair, thinking of how she used to comb it and put on lipstick and a clean blouse before he came home at night. But lately, especially when she was on a writing binge, she wore the same old sweats or t-shirts and shorts day in and day out. And she hadn't used makeup in months.

A flash of light caught her eye. Marie twisted to see flames in the dining room, just beyond the living room archway. Oh, no! Dan was asleep upstairs.

She dashed across the porch and flung open the screen door. "Dan, wake up!" Charging through the living room, she shouted, "Dan, you've got to get—"

Marie stopped. A glittering crystal rose bowl ringed with red roses sat in the middle of the dining room table, reflecting and refracting the light of a solitary candle. Palms against her pounding heart, she checked the room. This was it? No fire?

A flower-bordered envelope lay beside the candle. Her name was written on it in Dan's square, bold print. Her heart raced. Why would he write her a letter? He didn't even like to write checks. Was he planning to leave her but afraid to tell her to her face? With shaking hands, she slowly opened the envelope and slid out a matching sheet of perfumed paper.

Follow the moonbeam to find the one who loves you most.

What? Marie rotated in a mindless circle. Moonbeam? What moonbeam? The one on the porch?

She read the note again. It couldn't be from Dan, even though it looked like his writing. He never talked mushy, and he'd never written her love notes. She sucked in a breath and did another three-sixty. Was this some kind of prank?

There it was. A crisscross swath of moonlight led from the dining room floor, across the sunroom, to the French doors that opened onto the patio but were now closed. Treading the light-path, she tiptoed to the doors and stopped. "Oh, my..."

Dressed in his best shirt and pants, her burly blue-collar husband leaned against the deck railing with posed casualness. He appeared to be moon-gazing. Nearby, a huge basket of red roses and two tall white candles topped a small linen-covered table.

Marie cracked the door open and heard music. Where was that coming from?

Dan turned to her. "Welcome, my love."

She gaped at him.

He smiled. "Sweetheart, please. Come join me."

She couldn't move. Not a finger, not a foot.

Dan walked to her, put his arm around her shoulders and guided her to the table, where he pulled a chair out and helped her sit. The soft melody seemed to emanate from somewhere near her feet and mingle with the scent of roses.

"What, what is...?" Thoughts washed from her brain before she could speak them.

Dan carefully poured amber liquid into wine glasses she recognized as the ones they'd used to toast each other at their wedding reception. "What's going on?" He chuckled. "Is that what you were trying to ask?"

She nodded.

"You must think I've lost it."

Marie opened her mouth, but no words came.

"Actually..." His forehead creased. "I thought I was about to lose *you*." He sat down and reached for her hand. She saw candlelight reflected in his eyes, which were bright with tears.

"You probably won't believe this..." He blinked and cleared his throat. "I talked with the company counselor about us."

She frowned.

"Don't worry." He raised his free hand. "I didn't tell him anything personal. I just asked how to improve our communication. He gave me several tips. And then..." Dan wiped tears from his cheeks. "Crazy as it sounds, he said, 'Isn't your wife the one who writes the romance novels?'"

"How?" Marie could barely croak the words out. "How did he know?"

"I guess his wife is quite a fan of yours. He asked if I'd read your books. I was embarrassed to have to say I hadn't. That's when he eyed me over the top of his glasses, like my grandfather used to do, and said, 'Dan, I have a feeling you'll find all the ideas you'll ever need right under your nose.'

"So I snuck a book from your shelf. I've been reading a chapter a day while I eat my lunch." He grinned. "Marie, you're a great writer. I've gotten so caught up in the story I can't wait for lunch time. And I want to read your other books, too."

She sat back, slowly shaking her head.

He squeezed her hand. "I know this is late in coming,

but I regret how much time I spend at work. I've missed you, and I want us to be friends and lovers again. I want to have fun, to do things and go places together. I want to work less and be with you more. To have long talks like when we were first married." He took a long breath, his chest rising with the effort. "Sorry. I'm not used to talking so much."

Now the tears rolled down her face. "That's what I want, too, sweetheart. More than anything in the world."

Dan lifted her fingers to his lips. "I love you."

"I love you, too." She caressed his jaw.

He wrapped her fingers around the stem of one of the goblets before picking up the other one. "Let's drink to us."

Marie clinked her glass against his. "May we have many more wonderful years together." Elbows touching on the table and arms intertwined, they sipped, smiling into each other's eyes.

They lowered their drinks, and Dan shoved a cereal bowl filled with chocolate-coated pretzels to Marie's side of the table. "Here, have some of these."

"Oh, Dan. My favorite. How sweet of you."

She slipped a pretzel between her husband's lips and ate one herself. Then Dan pulled her to her feet to kiss her long and hard. Giggles from the direction of the twins' house finally drew them apart.

Dan raised an eyebrow. "Must of trimmed the bushes too low."

"That's okay." Marie grinned. "Maybe they can learn a thing or two from us old fogies." She laid her head on his chest. "Can I borrow that line?"

[89]

"What line?"

They began to slow dance to the music.

"The one about following the moonbeam."

Dan groaned. "I know, I know. It's corny. But you have only yourself to blame. Reading your book makes me feel poetic."

"It's perfect." She snuggled closer. "Especially the part about finding the one who loves you most."

———————

TANGLED

Valerie D. Gray

I'd only been in bed a few minutes when the latch on my bedroom door clicked. I yanked the covers to my chin and squeezed my eyes closed. Maybe this time my stepfather would think I was asleep.

The floor squeaked twice before I felt his hot breath on my cheek. I didn't move.

"I know you're awake." Richard's voice was low, but I heard the anger that always simmered beneath his stony exterior, like a shark lurking in calm water. "Roll over."

Through narrowed lids, I saw his burly silhouette outlined by the hall light—and the glint of a belt buckle in his hand. I squeaked, "I'm trying to sleep."

He ripped the blanket from my grip. "You deserve this, so stop your whimpering."

"I'll go to sleep faster, I promise." I tried to grab my covers back. "Please don't spank me."

He flipped me like a pancake. "Too little too late."

I screamed and scooted as far from him as I could get. "Mama, help!" I don't know why I yelled for her. She'd never before protected me from her husband.

Richard shoved me into the wall. Howling like an animal, he whipped my arms, my legs, my back and my bottom, again and again.

I curled into a ball. "Stop, please stop," I cried. "I'll be good."

The ceiling light flashed on, and I heard my mom say, "Richard, leave her alone."

"You stay out of it."

At the sound of a slap and a thump, I rolled over to see what happened.

Mom was slumped against the wall, staring at Richard. "You hit me." She sounded surprised. Then she started to cry.

He reached for her. "I didn't mean to hurt you."

She pulled away.

He swung around, glowering at me. "Now, look what you did." Then he ushered my mother out of the room, turned off the light and slammed the door shut.

Later that night, while I was still awake and crying silently into my pillow, my stepfather entered my room again. I began to tremble. He'd come back to finish what he started. But he just stood beside my bed. Although I lay as still as I could manage, I knew he knew I was awake. Somehow, he always knew.

Finally, he spoke. "Things got out of hand tonight, Karen. I...I'm sorry. But you must be a good girl and not upset me again." With that, he left the room.

I was relieved to know there would be no more beatings that night, but it was small comfort. If I could have been good enough to keep from making Richard angry, I would have tried even harder to please him, but *good enough* was impossible.

My stepfather beat me well into my teen years. By that time, I'd developed my own brand of rage, seething under my breath every time he accused me of something I didn't do. I constantly lied to him because he never believed the truth. I was insecure, unhappy and unloved, and I attempted to escape my misery through drinking, drugs and friends.

One perfect summer evening, my girlfriends and I hosted a party to celebrate our eighteenth birthdays. The night air was warm and filled with the sound of music and laughter—and the smell of alcohol. The party got wilder as the night wore on. After midnight, the dancing spilled out into the street, but I sat at the makeshift bar in the front yard, talking with one friend after another.

I couldn't believe it when Steve Reynolds sat down next to me. He was popular and cute, and older than I was. He had brown eyes that twinkled. No kidding. It was like there was light behind his eyes.

He smiled, and my heart did a little dance. "Hey," he said, "I hear you're one of the birthday girls." He held up his Coke bottle to toast me. "Happy birthday!"

I'd never done a toast before, but I lifted my Coke, just like in the movies, and we clinked our bottles together. "Thanks."

We talked for a while. He was sweet and fun and sort of shy, but that didn't stop him from teasing me. After a bit, he finished his drink and put it down. "I'd better hit the sheets if I'm going to make it to church in the morning."

I hated for our conversation to end, but I said, "Yeah, it's getting late." I motioned toward my friends, who were still singing and dancing in the street. "I'm afraid the neighbors are going to call the cops if those guys don't quiet down."

He spun on his stool and stopped so that he faced me. "Hey, why don't I pick you up in the morning and take you to church with me?"

I was so surprised I choked on my drink. Somehow, I managed to say, "I guess I could do that."

He helped me out of my chair but continued to hold my hand, which seemed to buzz where his skin touched mine.

"What time?" I asked. I tried to act cool, but inside, I was jumping up and down, thrilled to be going out with him. Church wasn't my thing, but I was more than willing to go anywhere Steve Reynolds asked me to go.

"Starts at ten. I'll pick you up around nine-thirty, if that's okay with you." He looped his arm in mine. "I'll walk you home. You live a couple blocks from here, right?"

"How'd you know?"

He winked. "Good guess."

I grinned, despite my fear I might not be able to walk a straight line. Though I'd only drunk soda pop, I felt intoxicated. As we left the party arm-in-arm, I nonchalantly waved goodbye to my girlfriends. Shock and maybe a hint of jealousy were written all over their pretty faces.

When we reached my front door, Steve gave me a gentle hug and said, "See you in the morning."

I didn't sleep much that night.

The church service was surprisingly enjoyable. I began to go every week, even when I knew Steve wouldn't be there. Soon, the Lord showed me how much I needed Him, and I asked Him to come into my life. He forgave my sins, filled me with His love, and made me His child. Hope flooded my poor hungry soul. For the first time in my life, I knew that somehow I'd be okay.

I discovered God promised peace and protection in the Bible, and I drank up His Word like the thirsty soul I was. I began to trust Him and know Him. He was more real to me than anyone I'd ever known. I could tell Him anything, and He listened. I learned to listen, too, and over time, my sassy, rebellious heart was healed. I became a different person.

My stepdad watched all this. One day, I came home to discover my pastor sitting in the living room with him. I hated to think what Richard had been telling him about me and was about to head straight for my bedroom, but he motioned for me to join them. To my amazement, the pastor was showing Richard in the Bible how to become a Christian, something I never dreamed possible.

I sat down between the two men and witnessed the amazing moment my stepfather asked Jesus to save him. From that point forward, our relationship was changed. It wasn't perfect, but Richard never beat me again, and I never sassed him again.

––––––––––

Even after Steve and I married and had children, horrible scenes from my childhood haunted me at night. Worse yet, I discovered I harbored the same anger and lack of self-control my stepfather had. Oh, I didn't beat my kids. In fact, I was quite lenient with them because I was afraid I'd follow in Richard's footsteps. On nights when I didn't have the patience to deal with a screaming infant, Steve graciously walked the floor with him or her.

One night when he was tending the baby, I fell asleep and had another nightmare. I think it was my pounding heart that awakened me. I rolled over and slowly breathed in and out, trying to calm myself. Why couldn't I forget the past?

My mom had long since divorced Richard. Even so, she and I didn't talk much. I felt abandoned by her, and I hadn't known my real father. My stepdad, Richard, was the only parent still involved in my life, if only at birthdays and holidays. My life was tangled and strange.

"God," I prayed, "why do I feel like such a mess? There's got to be more. You didn't just save my soul for eternity, you died for my life here on earth, too." I was desperate for my heart to be healed.

Consumed with my thoughts, I didn't notice the baby's wails had quieted until the bedroom door opened and Steve tiptoed back into the room. He sat down next to me and took my hand in his. "Honey," he whispered, "you're crying." With gentle fingers, he wiped the tears away. "Let me pray for you." And he did. Again.

―――――――

The next morning, I was greeted by a perfect spring day filled with new possibilities. A friend had offered to keep our kids for a few hours, so I could work in my garden. When I returned from dropping them off, I poured myself a glass of iced tea and sat on the front porch, watering my flowers and enjoying a moment of solitude interrupted only by birdsong.

I closed my eyes to soak in the calm and the sun's warmth on my face. When I opened them, I saw a familiar car drive up the street and pull into our driveway. My heart lurched. *Richard.* What was he doing here? Why wasn't he at work? After all this time, I still felt uneasy in his presence.

I got up and went to the spigot to turn off the water. All the while, my heart was pounding my ribs. I watched him walk across the grass toward me. "Hey, Dad, what brings you here in the middle of the day?"

To my surprise, he embraced me in a bear hug, as if we hadn't seen each other in years. Finally, he stepped back. "I need to talk to you about something." His voice was husky, and sunshine reflected off unshed tears in his eyes.

My heart pounded even harder. "Is something wrong?"

He ran a shaky hand over his thinning hair. "That's why I'm here."

Why was he so mysterious? Was he ill? Maybe he had cancer.

Looking everywhere except at me, Richard opened his mouth, but then he closed it. After a bit, he cleared his throat. "Karen, do you ever beat your kids?"

What? I felt the hairs on the backs of my arms rise. "Why?" I asked. "Why do you want to know?"

He held up a hand. "I promise I'll explain later. Please tell me. This is important."

I stared at my bare feet as I shuffled them back and forth on the grass. "No, I never beat them. I give them lots of timeouts, and sometimes I spank them. But if I'm angry...if I don't trust myself, I wait for Steve to come home, or I send them to their room until I calm down."

I looked at him. "The calm comes easier these days.

[97]

God and my husband have helped me with my temper."

"Thank you. I just needed to know."

"What do you mean, you *just needed to know*?"

His neck turned red. "Last night..." The color spread upward. "Last night, my sister and I went to see our mother in the nursing home. We asked her about the times she beat the two of us. I couldn't believe it when she looked us in the eye and outright denied she'd ever hit us.

"We reminded her of how she used to smash our fingers with our school books. She insisted she never did such a thing. But I thought surely she'd remember throwing bricks at us. Instead, she said we had wild, evil imaginations."

"Oh, Dad. I had no idea."

A butterfly floated between us. He watched it flutter away before focusing on me again. "The fact she didn't remember hurt more than the memories. I, I don't want you to live with memories I might forget."

I folded my arms. I didn't care what he remembered or what he forgot. I just wanted to put the past behind me. "I'd rather not go there, Dad."

"Please, Karen. Please hear me out."

He looked so miserable that I said nothing more and steeled myself for whatever was coming next.

"Up until yesterday," he said, "I felt the same way. I thought it was best to let sleeping dogs lie. But I now know I was wrong."

I frowned.

He gripped my shoulders. "I don't want you to think I forgot what I did to you. I remember all of it, and I am so sorry. Will you please forgive me?" The tears finally released and rolled down his cheeks.

I was dumbstruck. Yes, I remembered the pain and suffering. But after so many years, I'd begun to wonder if the abuse really happened the way I remembered. As I stared into his sad eyes, blood rushed to my head, like I'd been turned upside down.

I smiled. "I forgive you, Dad." Immediately, I was back on my feet again. But this time, for the first time, they were on solid ground.

———————

"Hey there, sleepyhead, wake up."

I opened my eyes and looked up from where I was resting with my head on my arms at the foot of my stepfather's hospital bed. "Oh, hi, Dad. I must have fallen asleep." I stood and stretched. "Boy, it sure is good to see you awake. Thanks for the scare of a lifetime." I bent over to hug him and kiss his cheek.

Richard touched his temples. "I must need my glasses." He chuckled. "You look a bit fuzzy around the edges."

I found his glasses on the nightstand and handed them to him. "I've been here all night, so I probably do look rumpled and fuzzy."

"Who's home with your kids?" He put the glasses on. Peering at me, he said, "Isn't Steve at work?"

"The kids are all grown and married. No one needs me at home right now." I watched him try to figure things out. Had the stroke affected his memory? "Remember all those great-grandchildren you have?"

"Oh, yes, of course." He laughed a nervous laugh, like he'd been doing more and more when reminded of his forgetfulness. "That must be why you look a lot older than the last time I saw you."

"Gee, thanks, Dad. You sure know how to make a girl feel good about herself." I ran my fingers through my hair and pulled lip gloss from my purse.

"Oh, now, stop that. I'm just teasing." He pushed a button to raise the head of the bed.

I patted his arm. "Before I nodded off, I was watching you sleep. You looked like you were having a bad dream. Do you remember it?"

He looked away. "No, I don't remember a dream." But a tear collected in the corner of his eye and ran down his cheek.

I grabbed a Kleenex to dab his face. "Don't keep it inside. You know it's better to let out whatever's bothering you. What was it?"

He fidgeted with the bed covers. "Just a memory, that's all."

I sat in the chair beside his bed. "Tell me about it, Dad."

"It's about that day..." He looked at the ceiling. "The day I went to your house to ask you to forgive me for...well, you know." He glanced at me. "Do you remember that day?"

"I'll never forget it." I clasped his frail hand in both of mine. "That was an important day for me, even though I'd already forgiven you. God had been healing my heart for many years, touching each broken part and making all things new, just like He promised to do." Now I had tears of my own.

He grabbed a tissue and swiped at my cheeks. "Go on, honey. Tell me why that day was so important to you." But then he scowled. "After that, I wish you'd forget about it."

"I can never forget that morning. You know why?"

He shook his head.

"Don't you know?" I squeezed his hand. "That was the day you became my dad."

————————

GRAND CHAMPION

Peter Leavell

Morgan pulled her steer's furry head down to chest level to comb the hair between his big brown eyes. This was it. Her last time to care for Kyle. Blinking back tears, she brushed across his wide back and down his hip and moved to the other side. She'd already shined his hooves with shoe polish.

Above the fair and carnival noises, she could hear the auctioneer's voice through the arena loudspeaker calling for bids. In just a few minutes, Kyle would be the animal in the spotlight. He'd be sold to the highest bidder, and the new owner would haul him to the slaughterhouse tomorrow. She tried to push the thought from her mind, but as she fluffed the steer's tail, she felt panic rising in her chest.

When her fourth-grade class toured a meatpacking plant last spring, she'd recognized the pungent manure aroma that permeated the stockyards, but she hadn't been able to put her finger on the smell inside the building. The odor reminded her of old tennis shoes and seemed to grow stronger the deeper they shuffled through endless concrete hallways into the bowels of the plant. Was it blood...or death she smelled? Dread clashed with curiosity in her gut and threatened to unsettle her breakfast.

Finally, the group slowed to file through gray doors with eye-level windows held open by two tall men. Both wore long white aprons and had hairnets around their hair and beards. The boy in front of her snorted and elbowed his friend. Morgan rolled her eyes. Boys made fun of everything.

Once they entered the cold, sterile room, her classmates clustered in small groups on the cement floor. Their hushed conversations echoed between the high block walls. Morgan's friend Sarah whispered, "I asked my mom to let me stay home this morning, but she said this would be good for me."

"My dad said the same thing." Morgan looked around the room, all the while trying to ignore the dead cow hanging by one leg from chains attached to a track on the ceiling. She thought she saw the cow twitch, and even though she knew it had to be her imagination, she cringed.

From behind long, clear-plastic strips, another man with a hairnet on his head stepped into the room, greeted them and slid the animal close. When he explained that the cow was not dead but had been rendered unconscious by an electrical shock to the head, a chill shot through Morgan. *The cow was still alive. The man was going to kill her, right in front of them.* She spun around and slipped to the back of the group.

The butcher pointed his big knife at her. "Want to help?"

She shook her head.

The other men chuckled.

The man with the knife talked as he worked. First, he slit the cow's throat. Morgan moaned. She was sure she saw the animal shudder, but everyone else seemed focused on the blood that drained from the gaping wound into a grate in the floor.

Next, he split the abdomen open to remove the intestines. Morgan tried to listen, but her attention was riveted on his apron. Like time-lapse photography on high speed, the cloth was quickly transformed from white to bright red, all the way down the front. She'd learned in science class that life was in the blood. Before their eyes, the cow's life was draining out of it. When the butcher began to skin the animal, three of the kids, a boy and two girls, threw up, and an aide took them to the bus.

The man waited until the other men cleaned up the mess and he had everyone's attention again before he continued his lecture. He told them that after they left, an employee would slide the carcass along the ceiling rail to the cooling room to be aged for a minimum of two weeks. During final processing, the beef would be quartered and the meat cut into steaks, roasts and stew meat or ground into hamburger.

Brandishing his knife, the butcher concluded with, "And that, boys and girls, is where your meat comes from. The next time you bite into a double-decker hamburger with all the trimmings, be sure to thank the cow who sacrificed her body for you."

More than one person had groaned after that comment. Morgan was one of them. She could still see the solemn expressions on her classmates' faces when they loaded onto the bus to return to school. They'd all lost a bit of innocence that day.

Following the tour, she'd done some research to find out what dying was like for cattle in slaughterhouses. One source said insufficient amperage—she'd had to look up both words—could paralyze an animal, but it would still be aware of what was happening and feel pain. She'd also learned that hanging heavy cows by one leg often caused their bones to break. Morgan had tried not to think about the terror of dying tortured and alone, but she couldn't stop herself from imagining their agony.

She sighed and leaned against her steer's broad cheek. He was destined for a horrible death. "I'm so sorry, Kyle. There's nothing I can do."

She heard the gate clink and lifted her head.

Her father stepped into the pen. "What are you doing, Morgan?"

She looked away.

"I told you not to name him." He dropped to one knee and took her hand. Eye to eye with his daughter, he said, "I know how difficult this is for you, but you need to learn we raise beef for food, not pets." He pulled a bandana from his back pocket and wiped tears from her face. "We can't get attached to the animals. It's just too hard when it comes time to let them go."

He squeezed her shoulder and stood. "Why did you name the steer after your brother?" Before she could answer, he said, "Kyle is gone, Morgan, and he's *not* coming back. Your mother and I have both discussed this with you."

She didn't respond.

Someone screamed, "Let me off!" followed by the

sound of the rollercoaster barreling to the bottom of the first slope.

Her father blew out a long breath. "I know you blame me for his death, Morgan, but it wasn't my fault. Kyle fell from the hayloft."

She wanted to tell her dad she didn't blame him, but the words wouldn't come. As for the name, she was just trying to keep her brother's memory alive.

He knelt before her again. This time his expression was stern. "You will walk that steer out there, you will watch him be auctioned off, and you will use the money you receive to buy more cattle. Do you understand me?"

Tears running down her face, all she could do was nod. Finally, she said, "I don't want him to go to the butcher."

"Has to, or the steer can't be sold to the grocery store." He got to his feet. "Health codes." Looking at Kyle, he said, "The steer looks great, ready to show. They'll be calling for him before long, so get him over to the arena pronto."

As soon as he left, Morgan threw her arms around Kyle and sobbed into his firm yet soft neck. Not long after the slaughterhouse tour, she'd run away from home, traveling down the river with the steer ambling behind her. Although he slowed now and then for a bite of grass, Kyle didn't need a rope. He had followed her everywhere he could since he was a calf.

When they stopped for the night, she'd slept on the ground snuggled up against his solid frame. The next morning, a deputy found them and called her dad, who brought a stock trailer and took them both home.

Kyle shifted.

Morgan straightened and wiped her face with her shirtsleeve. Selling her steer wouldn't be so bad if she knew he would die peacefully and painlessly. She dried his neck with a towel and re-combed the hair. How could she make sure he didn't feel the knife slice through his throat and death creep into his body?

She considered bribing the butcher, like she'd learned in history class. Men facing firing squads sometimes paid the shooters to aim for the heart so they'd have quick, painless deaths. She could use the money she earned from Kyle's sale. But what if her father found out? And where would she get the money for more livestock?

She studied the steer. He munched hay as if he didn't have a care in the world. What if she ended his life herself? Her dad had a .22 pistol in his truck. If she held it close to Kyle's head, she could end his life quickly, without pain. Her brother had told her that's what her father did when he put their old dog down.

Morgan whispered, "I love you, Kyle," and kissed his cold nose. One last hug and she ducked between the bars to scurry through the barn and past the crowd on the bleachers. She ran to where her father stood on the dusty sidelines. The big overhead lights made the arena brighter than day, but the bull on the auction block didn't seem to notice.

Her dad put his arm around her shoulders. "You okay?"

She nodded and forced a smile. "I'm good, Daddy. I can do this, but I forgot to check my hair. Can I have the truck key? I left my comb in the glove box."

He grinned. "You look fine, darling..." Digging into the front pocket of his jeans, he retrieved the keys and handed them to her. "Here you go." He pulled back his shirtsleeve to expose his watch. "Don't forget you have to show in a few minutes."

"I'll be right back."

Morgan hurried through the dim parking lot, winding between vehicles to her dad's old pickup. She shoved a key into the lock on the passenger side, but it didn't work, and neither did the next key. Maybe it was because her hands were shaking.

She fumbled for another key and dropped the whole set. Falling to her knees, she ran her hands across the gravel. She had to hurry. The auctioneer was calling for the next steer. Finally, she found the keys and jumped to her feet. The first one she tried worked. She flung the door wide, opened the glove compartment, and grabbed the gun.

Morgan looked around. No one could see her. Even so, she was thankful the interior lights in her dad's old truck didn't work. She tucked the pistol into the front of her pants, pulled her shirt over it, and hustled back to Kyle. Her father stood outside the pen, leaning against the rail.

She folded her arms across her midsection. Had he seen the bulge?

He held out his hand. "Your hair looks worse than before."

Morgan shrugged and dropped the keys on his palm.

He gave her a funny look. "See you at the arena." And then he left.

She slid a halter over Kyle's head, clipped his grand champion ribbon to the side of it, and snapped on the lead rope. Together, they left the pen and made their way through the barn that smelled of manure and straw. Walking with a gun in her pants felt weird, but she had to do what she had to do.

Two cows mooed as they passed by. She imagined they were wishing her steer good luck. He returned the greeting.

Morgan reached the chute and took a deep breath. She could see her parents seated in the front row of the stands. All around them sat business owners prepared to bid on her grand-champion steer. The price would be high. Whoever purchased the champion would be mentioned on the evening news and featured in a front-page article in the newspaper.

Other children cried when their animals were sold. They didn't have a plan like she did. Kyle's death would be on her terms, not the butcher's. She patted her steer's neck. She'd miss telling him her troubles and his sweet look that said everything would be all right. But those talks would end tonight, along with Kyle's life. Morgan pressed her lips together. This was not the time to lose control.

Her name was called. She walked into the ring with Kyle close behind. They approached the three auctioneers, who stood on the auction block. One did the talking and the other two helped spot the bidders. They were telling jokes and making fun of each other but quickly switched to praising the grand-champion steer. They pointed out his muscle and perfect form and emphasized his good breeding.

Morgan turned Kyle one direction then another so the bidders could get a good look at him. Kyle chewed his cud and ignored the crowd, oblivious to the death sentence about to be passed.

The auctioneer started the bidding at two thousand, and the war began. He buzzed prices off his lips so fast Morgan wondered how anyone could understand him.

The grocer nodded, and one of the helpers erupted with a "hey!"

Morgan held her breath. *Oh, please, not the grocery store owner.* Her family shopped at his store. The auctioneer continued the buzz, looking this way and that for potential buyers. The helpers pointed into the crowd, calling for bidders. "Hey!" they cried in unison as a trucker raised a finger.

When would be the right time to do it? Morgan prayed she'd know the exact instant. One bullet or two? Better make it two, right after the auctioneer yelled, "Sold."

The bids stopped. She tensed. Going once, twice, to the trucker. The grocer lifted his chin, and an auctioneer shouted, "Hey!"

She swallowed.

The bank owner cleared his throat and upped the bid.

Morgan felt the pistol press against her belly. Still holding Kyle's lead rope, she adjusted the gun with her other hand.

The bidding slowed at ten thousand. The grocer nodded again, bringing the price over ten thousand. The auctioneer pointed at the bank owner, saying "eleven thousand" over and over so fast he sounded like a hummingbird. The banker coughed, and the crowd buzzed with excitement.

Now that there were only two interested parties, the helpers were no longer needed. The main auctioneer pointed to the grocer. Eleven five, the auctioneer insisted. "C'mon. Eleven five. C'mon."

The man lifted a thumb, and the crowd applauded. Attention turned back to the banker. Morgan pleaded in her heart for him to raise the bid. The auctioneer shouted,

"Twelve. C'mon. C'mon. C'mon. Twelve." The banker coughed. Back to the grocer. "Twelve five. Twelve five. You got twelve 'n a half?" A dip of the head. The crowd cheered as all turned back to the banker.

"C'mon, thirteen. Take this deal, c'mon."

Morgan bit her lip. *Please*.... The crowd was silent, all eyes on the banker. Finally, a soft head shake, and the crowd sighed as one.

"Thirteen?" The auctioneers searched the bleachers for a new bidder. No one moved. No one dared move.

"Once, twice, sold! This year's grand-champion steer is sold to the grocer!" The crowd clapped.

Now, Morgan told herself. She kissed Kyle on the nose and felt her courage slip—until the image of him hanging by one leg filled her vision. "I love you, Kyle." She lifted her shirt and pulled out the pistol.

A woman screamed.

Holding the gun with both hands, Morgan turned toward her.

Someone yelled, "She's got a gun!" and people began to leap off the bleachers, scrambling to get away.

Morgan turned. As she did, she noticed the crowd on the other side separating. She twisted the gun sideways to flip off the safety, and more onlookers ran. Like a wave, wherever she pointed, people parted. All three auctioneers headed her direction. She aimed the gun at them, and they retreated under the bleachers.

She swung around. Kyle stood before her, patient as always. She leveled the gun at his head, but just as she was about to pull the trigger, strong arms wrapped around her, dragging her off the auction block. The gun fell from her hands and skidded in the dust.

Kyle watched her go. She screamed and called his name, but he just looked at her.

She kicked her captor, clawing at the hands that held her in an iron grip. Hearing a loud pop, she glanced up in time to see Kyle collapse on the arena floor in a billow of dust. Her father stood above the steer, the .22 in his hand.

"What in tarnation?" The one who held her relaxed his grip.

Morgan ran to her father.

He dropped the pistol and wrapped his arms around her.

Through her tears, she whispered, "Thank you, Daddy," and peered up at his careworn face. She saw the sadness in his eyes. And she knew. Her dad missed her brother as much as she did.

He wiped her tears from her cheeks. "There's only so much sadness one heart can handle." Pulling her close, he held her until the world no longer mattered. Until their hearts beat as one.

———————

THE GOD GIFT

Rebecca Carey Lyles

Keturah tossed one last withered stick into the basket and stooped to lift it to her shoulder. She swayed as she straightened, dizzy from the heat and an empty stomach. Would there ever be an end to this miserable drought?

She surveyed the barren landscape around her. Almost all of the shriveled shrubs in the wasteland between Zarephath and the Great Sea had been stripped for firewood. Each time she ventured outside the city to search for fuel, she had to walk farther into the desert to find more twigs. She glanced back to where her son, Bershi, was playing with rocks beneath the long shadow of Zarephath's high wall. From this distance, she could barely make out his small form. She hated to leave him so far behind, but she didn't want the sun to drain what little energy he had.

A dust devil swirled over the scorched earth, gathering sand and dirt and flinging it into the sky, its path unobstructed by trees or structures. Soon her people would be forced to forage the Lebanon Mountains for wood. But few would have the strength to walk that far or make the climb.

And what good would wood do without food to cook? If only she and Bershi could flee the famine. But she'd heard there was no escape in all of Phoenicia. She shoved at a pebble with her sandaled toe. Life had not been easy since her dear Joatham's death. Even before the rains stopped, she'd struggled to provide for her son and herself. But now...

Keturah adjusted the basket, which was digging into her bony shoulder. Today, she would bake their last bread cake—and no one cared. A bitter sob rasped from her dry throat. Baal, their supposed deity of rain and bountiful harvest, the lord of life itself, ignored her pleas for mercy, just like he did when Joatham was ill.

Despite her weakness, Keturah squared her shoulders and lifted her head. She might be at death's door, but she would not, could not pacify that cruel god by sacrificing another child. Bershi was her only reason to live.

A movement in the distance caught her attention. Keturah squinted. A dark figure was plodding toward her. Miniature dust clouds followed each footstep.

Hair rose on the back of her neck, and Keturah sucked in a breath. She'd lived this moment before. It would be a man. Shading her eyes with her free hand, she watched the traveler draw closer. Yes, definitely a man. She recognized the way he marched along, his head high, a walking stick grasped in one hand.

She blinked and rubbed her eyes. Hunger and heat were affecting her mind. Even so, a chill shot through her hot body. Last night's dream had been so real, so vivid. And now, she was seeing it reenacted. Or maybe she was hallucinating. She slapped her cheek and felt the sting.

The voice from the dream spoke again. "Feed my prophet."

Keturah looked around but saw no one other than the stranger. What was happening to her?

The muscular man strode through the coarse sand without altering his pace. She wanted to turn and run, but she couldn't tear her gaze from his raven eyes. Dirt crusted his entire body, from his long, shaggy, black mane and straggly gray-streaked beard to his well-worn leather sandals. His scant camel-hair garment was anchored by a wide cowhide belt. Thick hair coated his arms and legs.

The man came to an abrupt halt in front of her. "I am Elijah from Tishbe in Gilead," he declared, shattering the desert stillness with his harsh voice.

Keturah jerked backward and almost dropped her basket.

"I come in the name of Jehovah," the stranger continued, "the All-Knowing, Almighty God of Israel." He smelled like he hadn't bathed in weeks, maybe months.

She stared at him. Why was he talking about a god?

"My journey has been long and hot," he continued, gazing beyond her and through her at the same time. "Jehovah said I would find a widow, one to whom he has given instructions concerning me, gathering wood outside the gates of Zarephath." His black eyes focused on her. "Are you that woman?"

Keturah's instinct was to deny the dream, grab her son and run from the wild man. Instead, she answered truthfully. "I am." Her voice quavered. "My husband was

Baal-Joatham. My name is..."

"Baal." The man pounded the hard desert floor with his walking stick. "Baal is a false god, an evil god—a demonic spirit from the pit!" He lowered his voice to a gritty growl. "And a baby killer."

Keturah gasped and glanced toward the city. If the guards heard him—

"I am Elijah," he repeated. "A prophet of the living, loving, eternal God." The frenzied man looked away, smiled vaguely and relaxed his grip on the walking stick. "I come in peace."

"May, may your god grant you everlasting peace." She shifted her heavy burden to her other shoulder.

"He will grant peace when we rid ourselves of Ahab and that wicked Baal-worshiping woman, Jezebel, spawn of your vile land." Elijah whirled and tramped toward the city wall.

Keturah shivered, hating to think what the city rulers would do to him if they learned of his blasphemy. Trailing cautiously behind, she followed Elijah into the shade, where he plopped down against the wall and said, "Please bring me a cup of water."

Despite his crude behavior, Keturah could not refuse a thirsty man—one who'd just walked untold miles through the desert. "Zarephath's wells are not yet dry. Rest here. I will return with water."

Bershi, who was nearby, joined them. "Mama, who's that man?"

"A traveler." She reached for his hand and turned to go.

"Your name?"

She hesitated but finally told Elijah her name.

"Keturah..." He pushed tangled hair from his tired face. "Bring me a piece of bread, too." His voice had lost its gruffness and was almost pleading.

Bread? The nerve of this foreigner. He insults my dead husband and our god and then asks for bread. Can't he see we're starving? She glared at him. "I swear by your god I haven't a single piece of bread in my house. I have only a handful of barley flour left and a little cooking oil in the bottom of the jug." Her voice came too loud and too fast and burned her parched throat.

She swallowed. "I have gathered a few small sticks to cook our last meal. Then my son and I will die."

Bershi gaped at her with wide eyes.

Keturah touched his shoulder, instantly regretting she'd spoken so bluntly in his presence.

Elijah's features softened. "Do not be afraid. Go ahead, bake a small loaf and bring it to me. There will be flour and oil left for you and your son. The Lord God of Israel promises you will have plenty of oil and meal in your pots until He sends rain and the crops grow again."

Keturah nearly dropped her basket. What had she gotten herself into? He was a madman. An urge to throw her sticks at the stranger and flee with Bershi into the safety behind the city gates pulsed through her.

But Elijah closed his eyes and leaned back. Even though he appeared unconcerned, she had a feeling he was aware of the strife within her spirit.

"Mama?" Bershi looked from her to Elijah and back with large, troubled eyes. "Are we really going to die?"

The wind shifted and Keturah caught another whiff of Elijah's body odor. She coughed to keep from gagging.

"We'll talk about it later. Right now, we must hurry home."

She grabbed her son's hand and rushed toward the portal, her mind whirling. *Our last meal and the prophet wants—demands—it for himself.* She could go without eating. What did one more meal matter? But how could she deny her only child a few more precious hours of life?

Bershi stumbled and almost fell. Keturah slowed her pace on the narrow street. For a brief moment, she dared to hope. What if the man's god really was different than Baal? Would Jehovah help them? The Phoenician princess, Jezebel, had married the Israelite king, Ahab, yet the Phoenicians and Israelites served different gods. Was it possible for one god to be more powerful than the others?

They worked their way through a crowded intersection. A passing man with a long pole balanced on his shoulder knocked the basket from her shoulder and didn't even look back. Keturah and Bershi bent to pick up their few scrawny sticks. Rude men, fickle gods, crazy prophets. Maybe it wouldn't be so terrible to leave this worthless world after all.

When they arrived at their house, she set the basket on the ground, and Bershi began to stack the firewood in the outdoor oven. Keturah started the fire before she went inside to empty her pots of flour and oil, not daring a second glance into the depleted vessels.

She mixed the ground barley and oil with water, simple substances, yet more precious than anything except life itself. Kneading the dough for the small loaf didn't require much time, but when she finished, she held it in her palms, unable to part with her treasure.

What if the man was telling the truth? Their lives would be changed forever. But what if he was lying? What if he stole their last morsel of food?

She closed her eyes. Did it matter? They would die soon, anyway.

Bershi came running into the house. "The fire is hot, Mama."

She quickly shaped the dough into a flat, round loaf, placed it on a baking stone and handed it to him. He scurried out of the room with such enthusiasm she couldn't help but smile. Her son was a good boy. Joatham would have been so proud of him.

She chewed at her thumbnail. How could she tell Bershi he couldn't eat the bread once it was baked? And how could she forgive herself for taking sustenance out of her dying child's mouth to give to a stranger who was not only a madman but Jezebel's enemy? She could be killed for feeding him.

Maybe that's what she deserved for sacrificing her firstborn, her beloved daughter, Tirzah, into Baal's fiery hands—and Joatham had died anyway. She would never forgive herself. Keturah buried her face in her hands, but she did not cry. The rare occasions that she wept, she wept alone, after Bershi was asleep.

The little loaf was soon baked to a tantalizing golden brown. Keturah removed the stone from the clay oven and slid the bread onto a woven cloth in the center of the table. She breathed in the satisfying aroma. The barley cake smelled so good, and they were so hungry. Bershi leaned close to sniff the flaxen loaf, close enough she could hear his stomach rumble. He looked up at her with bright eyes.

Keturah had to look away. What if the Israelite god was as undependable as the Phoenician gods? What if giving away the last of their food killed her son? What if—?

"Can we eat now, Mama?"

Answering him was the hardest thing she'd done since she sacrificed her daughter. "Remember what that man outside the city wall said?" She touched his thin shoulder. "We must give this loaf to him."

Bershi's eyes widened. "But, Mama, I'm hungry." He clutched his stomach. "It hurts."

Keturah took her son's thin, dry hands. "I know, I know... But we have no more flour or oil." She hoped her smile covered the panic and desperation she felt. "That man and his god promised if we give the prophet the barley cake, we will have plenty to eat."

"I heard him say that, but..."

"This bread is only for today, Bershi. If we eat it, we eat our last meal. Then we will die, like your grandparents and your father...and your sister. But if we give the bread away, the prophet said his god will fill our pots with enough flour and oil for today and tomorrow, and as long as we need. We must believe him. We have no other hope."

———————

Elijah's raucous snoring greeted them when they neared the wall. Bershi tiptoed close and set the water jar beside the sleeping man. Keturah cringed when he tapped the prophet's filthy shoulder. "Wake up, prophet," Bershi said. "We brought you water to drink and bread to eat."

The hairy man lurched to a sitting position. He stared at them, his bird-like eyes dull and dazed.

Overwhelmed again by doubt and fear, Keturah threw

the basket at Elijah. "Take the last of our bread." She grabbed her son's hand and fled. They would die together, at home.

When they neared their house, Bershi broke from her grasp and burst through the doorway, but Keturah stopped to kneel beside the oven. She stirred the glowing embers, the remains of their final fire. Which of them would die first?

"Mama, Mama." Bershi's excited yell broke into her reverie. "Come quick."

Keturah jumped to her feet, almost passing out from the sudden movement. She darted inside the house to find her son standing triumphantly above the grain barrel and oil jug. With what had to be the last of his strength, he'd slid them before a window. "Look, Mama, look."

She peeked into the flour container and then the oil jar. "Oh, Bershi, he did it. The Israelite god did it." She pulled her child close, tears of joy spilling down her cheeks and onto his head.

"Let's dance." Bershi held out his hands.

Keturah laughed, and together, they twirled around the room until dizziness overcame them both. They fell onto a mat, gasping for breath. But a second later, Bershi was on his feet. "Time to cook." He tugged at his mother's garment before he ran out of the room, calling, "I'll stir the fire and add some sticks."

———————

Keturah opened her eyes.

Bershi was patting her face with a touch as soft as a breeze. "Wake up, Mama," he said. "We can make another cake this morning."

She smiled. The morning sun rarely had a chance to warm her son's cheeks before he rolled his pallet into the corner and threw on his tunic.

He hurried to the other side of the room to peek inside the tall jars. "Aha. Just enough for one loaf, maybe two."

"Come, Bershi."

He skipped to her side.

Keturah took his hand. "First, we must find Elijah to thank him and invite him to eat with us. After that, we will gather more fuel. Our flour and oil will not cook without a fire."

———————

Outside the city wall, Bershi pointed toward the Great Sea. "There he is."

Keturah nodded. "Yes, that has to be him." The stocky man's snarled hair and beard fluttered around his head and shoulders. She took a deep breath, savoring the salty early morning breeze that drifted off the water and dreading another encounter with the stench that emanated from the man.

"Give him your guest room."

"What?" Keturah whirled.

Bershi gave her a questioning look. "I didn't say anything, Mama."

The Voice spoke again. "Give him the room on your roof."

Keturah dipped her head. "Yes, Jehovah." She chuckled, amused by the familiarity with which she spoke, as if she'd been talking to the Israelite god all her life.

———————

From that day on, Keturah made barley cakes for her son and herself and their houseguest every day. Elijah was a man of few words, and those few words were often strident and condemning. Yet, despite his uncouth behavior, she knew she could trust him. He was Jehovah's messenger on earth.

Just when Bershi's bony arms had regained their childish contours and the drawn look had left his face, Keturah awakened early one morning to find him tossing and moaning on his pallet. His body was pink with fever and damp with perspiration, like Joatham's had been during his long sickness.

Her heart convulsed. What could be the matter? He'd been perfectly healthy the day before. She swallowed her fear, placed wet cloths on his head and tried to get him to drink water. Throughout the morning, he worsened. As she exchanged a hot cloth on his forehead for a fresh cool one, she whispered, "Bershi, I must go for help."

At that moment, he slipped into unconsciousness and stopped breathing.

"No." she cried. "Bershi, no..." She shook his limp body. He did not respond. Pulling him to her chest, she staggered to her feet, screaming, "E-li-jah, Elijah!"

Through a fog of panic, she heard the prophet race down the exterior stairs. When he rushed into the room, she yelled, "What do you have against me? Did you come to remind me of my sin?" Her voice was thick with anguish. "Is it because I sacrificed my child to the god you hate? Did you kill my son to punish me?"

Ignoring her accusations, Elijah demanded, "Give the boy to me." He snatched Bershi from her arms and dashed out of the house and up the stairs.

Keturah fell across Bershi's pallet. "My son, my son," she sobbed. "My only child..." She gripped the blanket in her fists. "Forgive me, Jehovah, for giving my daughter to the priests to kill. I was wrong, so wrong."

A loud lament from above made her sit up. In a mighty voice, Elijah pleaded, "Lord, why do you bring tragedy to this woman, the very one who has provided shelter and meals for me at your direction? Oh, my God, let this boy's life return to him."

Keturah held her breath. "Please, Jehovah..." She dug her fingernails into the pallet. "Please..."

A deafening stillness filled the room. She was about to collapse in defeat and grief, when she heard the rumble of footsteps on the outer stairs and Elijah burst through the doorway.

Keturah stumbled to her feet.

"Look!" Elijah thrust her boy into her arms. "Your son lives."

Tears streaming down her face, she kissed Bershi's soft cheeks again and again, ignoring his confused expression. Finally, she turned to Elijah. "I believe. I believe Jehovah is the only true God, a loving and generous God. You are His prophet, and you speak the truth. Forgive my doubt."

Keturah set Bershi on his feet and stood behind him, her hands on his shoulders to steady him. "I give my son, my only child, to Jehovah and to you as my offering of thanksgiving. He will be a good helper to you."

Elijah frowned.

Keturah raised her chin and met his gaze. "I don't want him to grow up in this blood-soaked evil land of hate and fear and death. That's all our hideous gods and goddesses and their depraved priests offer." She wrapped her arms around her son. "This is my sacrifice of love...love for Bershi, and love for Jehovah, the God of life and love."

———————

Bad Girl

Lisa Michelle Hess

On a Thursday afternoon, our town's small library is empty except for my librarian and me, which is good because her expression is equal parts concern and annoyance. But that's not the worst of it. I'm standing on the other side of the counter with obscenities about to burst from my lips like birds from a cage, and I'm wondering, how did I get here?

Somehow, I've ended up the leader of a women's book club. When I told my sister, she laughed so loud I had to hold the phone away from my ear. "Why do you do these things to yourself?" I pictured her shaking her head at me. "People stress you out," she said. "You should be living in a cabin on a mountain somewhere with no electricity and a phone you only have for emergencies. Instead, you end up with fifteen women and twice as many toddlers descending on your home once a week for scones, coffee and reassurance. Why do you let this happen to you?"

I didn't mean to. Just like I didn't plan to be standing here, staring at my librarian with some of the vilest words in the English language pounding in my brain to the rhythm of my ever-increasing heartbeat.

The women in my book group are in their twenties and thirties, with a couple of old girls like me who are in their forties and did careers first, then kids. They run the gamut of liberal and hipster-rich to extremely conservative and not so wealthy, from self-educated to multi-graduate degreed—which makes for some weird, cross-cultural discussions, by the way.

But generally, everyone is fairly accepting. We're all Christians, of one kind or another, so we have to at least act like we love each other. Most of the time, I think the affection is genuine.

I could be wrong, though. My sister knows me well. Intuition about human relationships is not my strong point, and these women could despise each other, for all I know. But they keep coming back, week after week, and I don't think it's just for the coffee.

One of the wealthy members, concerned for the not-so-wealthy ones, wanted to see if we could find some way to get our books for free. My poorer book club members never suggested they had trouble getting their hands on a book, but they took the gesture in the spirit it was offered.

We'd been reading this series called *The Bad Bible Girls* about women in the line of Christ who'd led less than exemplary lives—and our discussions were going well. The members had all warmed to the idea that God accepted and used imperfect, diverse women just like them.

Somebody learned that if we registered our book club with the local library, we could get copies for all of us and a longer check-out period. Great idea, everyone agreed. "However," liberal hipster-rich said, "we have to have a name for our group." That discussion took up the rest of the meeting, but everyone finally decided on a name.

The next day, I added a library visit to my long list of errands and kid carpools. All I had to do was run in, tell the librarian the name of our group and sign a form. How long could it take?

"Are you sure *that's* the name you want?" My librarian looked as if I'd just served her monkey brains.

She peered at me over her glasses, expecting a response, but I was caught off-guard. My hot, hungry, increasingly bored children were waiting in the car and was she really going to make an issue out of this? "Well, yeah, I'm sure." I didn't even try to disguise my impatience. "Everybody agreed to it."

I adore my book club friends, but navigating a course through their personalities can be treacherous. As my librarian's lips straightened into a disapproving line, I imagined the women in my group arguing about a more appropriate name as they changed the aromatic diapers of frustrated toddlers and nursed their wailing infants. *I don't think so.*

"You know, a lot of people in the system are going to see this name," the librarian said, as if I hadn't responded. "There's the woman at Central who handles the book clubs and my boss over in Smithton, just for a start. They list the names of all the book clubs in the newsletter, you know. I don't think they'll understand."

That was when my already tissue-thin patience

shredded, and my brain filled with *some language*, as they say in the movie guides. Really, those words rarely come out of my mouth. I *think* them all the time, though. I may not be of the world, but I'm in it, you know?

I can't understand why she cares so much about the admittedly inappropriate nature of the name we've chosen. I rack my brain, trying to make sense of this attitude I'm getting from her. Why these waves of criticism crashing toward me from across the desk?

I actually like this librarian. I consider her a friend of sorts. Her kids are about the same age as mine. We've had some good conversations at soccer games about kids, husbands, life. Her face with its frown of censure fades, and the dusty, musty smell of the library is replaced by the scent of loamy earth and wet grass.

I remember one particular evening I spent with her. We are leaning against our cars, watching the kids on the field, while dusk settles around us and mist beads on our fleece jackets. We discuss how much we love our families and our friends, but they wear us out. We cry and we laugh. We hug when we say goodbye.

But that was a long time ago. Her face comes back into focus, and my brain fills with those words that betray my lack of self-control, like they're plastered across her forehead. Before I completely lose it, I want to be finished with this. It's taking up too much time, as if the rest of my life isn't draining enough.

"Look." I practically yell. "That's the name." I stretch across the counter and jab at her computer screen with my finger. "Type it into the computer." I enunciate each word clearly. "*Bad. Bible. Girls.* That's what we are. Freakin' Bad Bible Girls!"

At that precise instant, the stern, white-haired president of the library board, of which I am also an officer, walks through the door with my three sweaty, forlorn-looking children close on her heels. They all stand there staring at us, mouths agape, eyes wide.

My librarian friend looks from them to me and turns to her keyboard. She shrugs and starts typing. "Okay," she says, a smirk tugging at the corner of her lips. "You're Freakin' Bad Bible Girls."

She covers her mouth to try to muffle the chuckle she can't contain, but it's no use. In seconds, we're both laughing out loud. The sound echoes through the library and fills it up. My kids join in, but the elderly member of our audience has a horrified expression on her face. I can see she's trying to decide which one of us to accuse of what.

If she picks me, I'll have no excuse. What can I say? I'm a bad girl.

———

THE MAGICIAN

Rebecca Carey Lyles

Seated on metal bleachers with two dozen other parents under a sweltering August sun, I fanned my face with a paper plate and watched Mr. Magic prepare to perform his final trick. He folded his arms and scanned the ten-year-olds clustered on the grass in front of his platform. "Who wants to be my last victim...er, volunteer?"

Our son punched his chubby hand high and frantically waved it above his head. Even though Joey had been passed over every other time the birthday party magician asked for a volunteer, he hadn't lost his enthusiasm. "Me, me. Pick me!" Like a metronome set on high, his waggling arm blurred in my vision.

From beneath his thick, black eyebrows, the man glared at the screaming children. Finally, he crooked a finger at Joey, who sprang to his feet, clambered onto the stage and spun around, hands on his waist. He stuck out his chest, as if proud of the green frosting smeared down the front of his new Iron Man t-shirt. Bright freckles flamed against his sunburned cheeks.

My husband, Roger, leaned close to me. "This should be interesting." The perspiration trailing down his temples glistened in the sunshine.

I pulled my sweat-soaked blouse away from my torso. "I hope he doesn't ruin the trick. Your son isn't exactly one to follow direction."

"If we're lucky, it'll go fast, and we can beat the crowd to Burt's Burgers." Roger dug a handkerchief from his back pocket and wiped his brow.

I lifted damp hair from my neck. "First thing I'll order is a large Pepsi with lots of ice."

The magician held his microphone in front of Joey. "What's your name?"

"Joey Hunter!" Our son's shout vibrated the metal stands we sat on, and onlookers covered their ears. They obviously had children who spoke in normal decibel levels. Joey hopped from one foot to the other. "What trick are we doing, Mr. Magic?"

Mr. Magic looked toward the bleachers. "Does Joey Hunter have a parent or a guardian in the crowd?"

Roger and I looked at each other and then raised our hands.

"This," proclaimed the magician, "is a *very dangerous trick*, the king of illusions. Do I have your permission to incorporate your son into the act?"

Joey grabbed at the microphone, missed and knocked it out of the man's hand. When it crashed to the stage, the loud crackle made everyone flinch. Before the magician could retrieve the microphone, Joey snatched it up and

[136]

shrieked, "Say 'yes'!"

Everyone turned to stare at us.

Roger shrugged. "What could be the harm?"

I whispered, "Mr. Magic didn't ask permission for the other tricks."

Roger leaned close. "It's part of the act, Susan, the build-up for the finale."

"Mom...Dad...come on," Joey whined, his nasal voice loud and distorted. Knowing Joey, his mouth was on the microphone.

Against my better judgment, I finally said, "Okay."

Roger gave the magician a thumbs-up. "Go for it."

Joey thrust his fist into the air. "Yes!" Arms flapping, he jumped up and down like a deranged turkey. On one of the upswings, the magician snatched the microphone from his hand.

His assistant rolled out a table from behind the curtain and helped Joey stretch across it. Then she turned up the volume on the boom box.

"Mr. Joey Hunter," called the magician, reaching into his Trunk of Tricks, "are you ready?"

"I'm ready, Mr. Magic!" His smile stretched from ear to ear, and his whole body quivered with anticipation.

A drum roll. A flash of reflected sunshine. A saw blade on our son's belly.

What? I gasped and grabbed Roger's arm.

In sync with the song's pulsating rhythm, the magician, with his assistant's help, pulled the saw back, pushed it forward, pulled back, pushed forward.

I wanted to scream, to tell the magician to stop mutilating my child. But I couldn't breathe, let alone speak.

Joey didn't flinch.

The music rose to a crescendo, and Mr. Magic swung the blade triumphantly upward. "Ta-da!"

Before I could process what the *ta-da* was all about, the assistant grabbed Joey's hips and legs and stood them upright.

"Oh, no..." The words squeaked from my throat, but Roger just grinned and patted my hand.

Mr. Magic slid behind Joey's head, grasped him under his arms and set him on his ribs. "Do a push-up."

Joey lifted himself with his arms—up, down, up, down—obviously pleased with the ease of the effort. He'd always preferred video games to exercise.

"Move your legs." One foot kicked out, then the other. Cries of disbelief bounced through the bleachers.

Joey's top half flipped off the table, shimmied down Mr. Magic's legs and hopped through the grass to climb a tree. His legs and feet did a little dance before skipping merrily after his upper body.

I jumped up. "We can't just sit here, Roger."

As the other horrified parents grabbed their children and ran for their cars, we headed for Joey's tree, but the legs ran away. I'd never seen our son move so fast. Roger pursued the fleeing half, and I parked under the tree branch. "Joey, sweetie, the party is over. Time to go."

He snickered. "Can't make me, Mom."

I clenched my fists. This was no time to get into my usual power game with our stubborn son. "Remember where we're going for lunch?"

The smirk faded. Food had always been Joey's

weakness.

"You can get the Super-Duper shake *and* double fries."

He swung off the branch and into my arms, nearly knocking me over. "Really?" His breath smelled like frosting.

"Really. Now let's go find your legs."

"But I like being two people."

"They won't let you into Burt's Burgers without the rest of your body."

Joey frowned. "Why not?"

"Remember the sign on the door? The one that says 'No Shirt, No Shoes, No Service'?"

"Yeah, so?"

"This part of you doesn't have shoes, and your bottom doesn't have a shirt."

His lower lip pooched. "Bummer."

We returned to the platform just as Roger offered the legs to Mr. Magic. "Time to put him back together."

The magician jutted his chin. "That'll cost you."

Joey wriggled in my arms, and his legs kicked at Roger. "I don't *wanna* go back together!"

I tightened my hold on his chest. "But, you just said..."

"I don't care what I said." He began beating on my forearms.

Roger stuffed Joey's lower half into a nearby metal trash can. I started to object, but Roger shook his head. "Just for a minute, to keep him contained." I could barely hear him over the sound of Joey's legs banging against the metal, like a cymbal player gone mad.

Someone needed to stop the craziness. I looked

around for the assistant, but she was nowhere in sight.

Roger grabbed our son's upper half from me and thrust it at the magician. "Fix him—now!"

Mr. Magic yelled above the racket, "What's it worth to you?"

Joey clawed at Roger's hands.

Roger swore, seized one of Joey's flailing arms and then the other and pinned them both to his torso. "That's enough, son. We have to go now—"

"No, no, no!" Joey looked like he was about to explode.

I reached for him, but Roger set Joey on the ground in front of the magician. When he straightened, a strange light illuminated his eyes. "What's it worth to *you*, Mr. Magic?"

The magician's eyebrows soared almost to his hairline. He stepped back.

Joey looked from his father to the magician and then back again. A slow grin spread across his smeared face. He lunged at the magician and clutched his leg. "I'll be the most fantabulous, super-awesomest, bestest assistant you ever had!"

Mr. Magic raised his palms. "Oh, no, I can't—"

Roger took my hand. "Let's go get that Pepsi, sweetheart. With lots of ice."

I kissed his cheek. "You must have read my mind."

———————

THREE DAYS

Peter Leavell

The ground trembled, sending shudders through Matt Wamer's chest. The engine was bearing down on him, its loud whistle echoing off the nearby fertilizer shed and grain silos. He laid a dime on the warm railroad track, but the vibrations threatened to dislodge it, so he repositioned it in the center of the rail and held it there as long as he could. Finally, he released the coin and backed away.

Hunkered down beside the railroad's rock bed, he watched the oncoming train curve toward him. A slight bend in the track gave him a good view of the long line of cars trailing behind. He was about to head for his usual hiding spot, when he stopped. *No, not today.* He'd stay close this time. A sixth-grader should take risks.

Perhaps fear would cut through the heartache. Three days ago, he'd helped lower his mother's coffin into a deep grave in the Penny Hill Cemetery. The constant ache in his head and chest had to end. But if he forgot his mother for even a second, guilt washed over him like a flash flood.

The earth shook, the train whistle bellowed, and a faint whiff of diesel pricked his nostrils. Matt's heart began to pound. He turned his back, holding his ears while the engine rushed by. A burst of wind struck him, nearly knocking him to his knees.

The sound of the horn was replaced by the thunder of steel wheels spinning and scraping against the rails. Boxcars and flatbeds clattered and clanged past and soon fell into a click-clack rhythm, telling the world, *She's dead...gone. She's dead...gone. Dead...gone.* He wished he'd counted the cars to distract his mind, but it was too late now.

The passing of the last car left a vacuum in the air. Amplified by the diminishing hum in the tracks, the sudden hush left him feeling bereft and forsaken. A cloud obliterated the summer sun. Matt sighed.

But then he remembered the dime and scrambled over the sharp stones to search for it between the railroad ties. Sunlight reappeared, and a gleam caught his eye. He reached down to pick up the smooth, flattened silver. The coin was slightly bent, like it had conformed to the wheel. He could almost make out Roosevelt's smashed face.

He checked the area for witnesses. His dad would have a fit if he knew he was playing on the tracks again. A lone, dark-haired figure stood by the fertilizer shed, watching him. He dropped the dime and shaded his eyes with his hand. "Mom?"

She stepped back and disappeared behind the shed.

Had he really just seen his mother?

Matt leaped across the track and plunged into the

ditch that ran alongside it. "Mom, wait!" Smashing through thick weeds, he charged up the other bank. Milkweed pods exploded around him and released their musky smell. His only thought to see his mother again, he sprinted across the gravel parking lot, vaulted over a concrete barrier and slid around a corner.

On the far side of the highway, his slender mother was slipping into the passenger seat of a car. The door slammed shut, and the back wheels sprayed gravel when the car took off. He ran after the vehicle, tripped and nose-dived into the dust. Ignoring the pebbles and thistles that bit into his arms, he sprang to his feet. But the car was already speeding down the highway.

Matt darted onto the road, calling and waving his arms until he could no longer see the vehicle. Finally, he sunk to the pavement and buried his face in his arms. He began to sob, crying harder than he'd cried at the funeral. She was gone, again.

He felt the asphalt's heat burn through his pants and jumped to his feet, wiping tears from his cheeks with the back of his hand. The whine of an oncoming vehicle penetrated his consciousness, but it wasn't until an air horn blasted close by that he stumbled to the shoulder. Horn still blaring, a semi-truck flew past, creating a wind gust almost as strong as the train's.

Matt didn't even blink.

Abandonment, loneliness and loss were now intertwined with confusion. He'd watched Harvey, the cemetery caretaker, bury his mother. She was dead. Yet... Matt staggered back over the ditch bank and railroad track to walk along a gravel road bordered by small square houses and tall cottonwoods. The corndog he'd microwaved and eaten an hour earlier rebelled, and a headache pounded against his forehead. He felt like every freckle on his face was drilling into his brain.

The sound of a crow cawing from a nearby telephone pole made his head hurt worse. He stuck his fingers in his ears and kept moving. The co-op's yellow single-story building was just ahead. Dropping his hands to his side, he hurried toward his dad's office. Maybe he would know what was going on.

He passed beneath an open window. Despite the rattle of augers shuffling corn from one of the co-op's massive silos into a truck, he heard his father say, "Get back here."

Matt stopped, thinking he'd spoken to him. But then he heard a woman giggle. "Not here, Arthur."

"C'mon, Darla, you know I'm grieving."

The secretary's voice was playful. "I can tell by your grip."

Matt heard a loud smack and another chuckle.

"Stop it, Arthur." Darla sounded serious. "You should be with your son. He's taking his mother's death hard. I can watch the office."

"And leave my little gal all alone? You'll..."

Matt crammed his fists in his pockets and started down Main Street. A car slowed and seemed to follow him. He looked up. It was Mrs. Johnson, his mom's friend. Her eyes were filled with sorrow and pity. "I'm sorry about your mom."

He nodded.

She smiled at him, and then she was gone.

He kicked a rock from the sidewalk into the street. The stone settled near the faded double line, somehow looking lonely all by itself in the middle of the street. Another car roared by. One of the tires caught the rock and sent it spinning away.

He lowered his head and tried to ignore the world but found he kept glancing around. Farm implement toys in the hardware store's window caught his attention. Beyond the display, a woman was chatting with Mr. Crowley, the owner.

Mom! Matt's heart raced. That's where she went after he saw her. He was about to open the door, when he realized the woman was Miss Morris, the first-grade teacher whose classroom was next to his mom's second-grade classroom.

Matt shoved his hand back into his pocket. Was he losing his mind? Miss Morris had brown hair like his mother, but she was shorter and younger.

All the way home, the afternoon's experiences played in his head over and over, until the woman he thought was his mother became a shrouded haze. Had he seen her ghost? He stared at the sky. The tire marks beside the road were real enough. The only answer was that he'd seen a real person. His mother was alive. But where was she?

The closer he got to his house, the stronger the feeling grew. Mom was alive. He knew she was. He marched up the steps and into the living room, letting the screen door slam behind him. Without pause, he picked up the telephone and dialed Ray's number. The rotary dial took forever to roll back to the zero after each number. Finally, the call went through, and his friend answered.

"It's Matt."

"You okay?"

"Yeah, look. I need help with something. Tonight."

Silence. Then, "Can it be tomorrow night?"

"Tonight, Ray. It's got to be tonight."

"Sure, okay. Tonight."

"Cool. Can I sleep at your place?"

"I suppose. I'll call you back if my mom says no."

Relief filled his chest. This was going to work. "Thanks. I'll be there soon. Oh, do you have a shovel?"

"Yeah, why?"

"I'll tell you later." Matt hung up the phone.

He wrote his father a note about the sleepover—like his father would care—and packed a duffel bag. Before leaving, he checked the refrigerator for food and found a solitary milk bottle. He drank half the milk, returned the bottle to the fridge and slipped out the back door.

———————

Ray's mom opened the screen door for Matt. Her straight black hair and generous smile caught him off guard and made him miss his mother. Tears threatened, but he choked back a sob and managed, "Ray home?"

"Come in, Matt." The look on her face was sad. "How are you doing?" More pity. Everyone seemed to feel sorry for him.

But not as sorry as he felt for himself. He hated that feeling and had to make it go away.

"I'm so glad you came over," she said. "Ray's in his usual spot. Head on up."

He walked down the hall to the stairs, passing the bathroom on the way. The smell of sweet, rotten wood filled his senses. Too much humidity in the Midwest is what his mother had told him. She was from Arizona, where the air was dry.

She'd also told him stories about the desert and the desperados and bandits who had hideouts in the canyons among the cactus and coyotes. He'd begged his dad for a family trip to Arizona—until his father slapped him, hard. From that point on, he'd kept his dreams hidden deep inside, like he did the loss of his mother.

He reached the top of the stairs. "Ray? You up here?"

"In my room."

Matt opened the door. Model glue vapor assaulted him like a smack in the face and made his eyes water even more. "Whoa." He stepped back.

Ray looked up from his desk, where he was working on a tiny airplane. "Man, you look terrible."

Matt ignored the comment and sat on the bed. "I need your help." He wiped his eyes with his shirttail. "You're not going to believe this, but..." He told Ray about seeing his mom and then explained his plan. By the time he finished, his fingers were numb, and he realized he'd been strangling Ray's pillow. "Will you help me?"

Ray nodded. "Of course."

"You believe me?"

Ray looked surprised. "Have you ever lied to me before?"

"No, but this is...different."

"Only one way to find out. Tonight?"

"Tonight."

———

Crouched behind a broad bush, Matt watched the night descend on Penny Hill Cemetery and hide everything but

[147]

the pale glow of scattered tombstones. The sound of rushing water and croaking frogs in the nearby river blocked all other noises, except for Ray's breathing. One by one, stars and fireflies twinkled to life and competed for Matt's attention, but he kept his focus on Harvey's trailer. Earlier, they'd seen him walk past an illuminated window.

Ray shifted, rattling the leaves in the next bush, and hissed, "He hasn't moved. Let's go."

"Wait. He guards the cemetery until he goes to bed."

"He's not guarding nothin'. My dad says Harvey just mows the lawn and picks up faded flowers."

"He guards the cemetery."

Ray sighed. "I gotta pee. Happens when I get nervous."

"No one's stopping you."

"Can't squeeze out a drop in the outdoors. You know that."

Matt sighed and wondered if he should have brought Brian instead.

Ray fell back in the grass. "What's next?"

The trailer lights blinked off.

Matt whispered, "Grab your shovel." He snatched up his own shovel, pushed out from the bush and stepped over a low stone wall into the cemetery. The night sky opened before him. Any other night, he would have fallen onto his back to study the wide expanse of stars above his head.

Instead, he pressed on. Maybe he was overreacting about Harvey staying awake. But the cemetery caretaker was also the school janitor. He had a way of outguessing their plans.

Despite the lack of light, Matt had no trouble finding his mother's plot in the small graveyard. The turf lines, which had been dug three days earlier, were still obvious.

Ray eyed the grave. "You think she's not there?"

"I have to know."

"What if...what if your mom *is* in there, Matt? What if there's worms and stuff?"

"Then we'll see worms." Matt positioned his shovel in the turf line and stomped down hard. The metal slid easily into the newly disturbed ground. He lifted out a chunk of grass and flung it to the side.

Ray stepped up beside him. "Okay, let's do this."

"Just dig in the front area. All we need is to be able to open the top half of the casket." Soon, they'd removed almost a cubic foot of the freshly turned soil. His arms warmed to the work as he flung dirt to the side.

From time to time, Matt looked up. First, their heads were level with the top of the new gravestone. After a bit, they were even with his mom's age, then her birthdate and death date. He could barely make out the chiseled numbers in the dim light.

His muscles began to burn. He'd been proud of his bulging biceps in school, showing them off to his friends and enjoying the reaction of the girls who watched from a distance. Now that he was actually putting them to use, his arms rebelled, but he ignored the pain.

When fatigue set in, he doubled his efforts and thought of his mother. Was she alive or dead? Would they learn the answer tonight?

The thick, rich smell of earth surrounded him, and the air in the hole was still and cool, which surprised him. He'd expected it to be warm, like the night air above ground, but he was grateful. The exertion made him sweat.

His breath came in gasps. "I think it's safe to use a flashlight now." Matt glanced at the moon. If only he could sit on the tiny sliver and watch the earth, see where his mother was, so he wouldn't have to dig a hole in a cemetery in the middle of the night.

The light switched on. He saw sweat trails on Ray's dirty face and felt the sting of salt in his own eyes.

"We've got to be close," Ray said. "My arms are about to fall off." He paused. "You hear that?"

"No, I didn't hear nothin'. Matt tossed a shovelful of dirt above his head and over the edge. "We're almost there."

Ray moaned. "Matt, I can't see out the hole."

Matt could tell his friend was shaking because the light was flickering.

"What if a hand reaches through the dirt and grabs me?" The light flashed wildly about the earthen walls. "God, help me," Ray rasped. "I'll be stuck down here forever." He felt for the holds they'd carved into the side.

"Quiet," Matt said. "We're almost there." He drove his shovel down and hit something solid. In the stillness of the night, the noise resounded like a gunshot.

Ray spun and churned at the dirt. "Gotta get out of here."

"It was just—"

Ray scrambled up the incline, dirt spraying behind him.

Matt lifted an arm to protect his face just as a wicked scream pierced the night. Ray fell back into the pit, crashing into Matt. They tumbled downward in a flurry of dust and groans.

A glaring light illuminated the hole brighter than day. Matt gasped. The beam was blinding. Could it be aliens?

"Who's in there?" The voice was gruff but human. It sounded like an old man...like Harvey.

"Don't kill us!" Ray pleaded. "Don't bury us alive!"

Dirt trickled down the side of the grave.

Heart pounding, Matt shoved Ray away and blocked the light with his hand. "That you, Harvey?"

"Matt? What in tarnation...? Why're you down there?"

Ray scrambled to his feet.

"Harvey," Matt pleaded, "you've got to let me finish."

The light moved to the side, illuminating the roots that drooped from the edge of the hole. "Come out of there, boys."

Matt couldn't hold back his tears. He had to find his mother. Sobbing, he gripped the shovel and scraped at the dirt, trying to get through the last few inches before Harvey stopped him.

The old man slid down in a shower of earth that left a dank taste in Matt's mouth. He ended his desperate scraping when Harvey straightened to full height in front of him. Holding a massive flashlight at his side, the old man reached out a hand, and Matt felt his boney grip on his shoulder. He looked up at him, and in the man's aged eyes, shriveled face and lean body, he saw something more than just pity. He saw hope.

"Harvey, I saw Mom this afternoon by the highway. I'm sure it was her." He hated the whine in his voice, but he couldn't help it. "Please let me finish. I've got to know."

The caretaker chewed at his bottom lip as if deciding what to do. "Sit up there." He pointed to the rim of the hole. "Both of you."

Harvey's words whistled and sounded funny, like he didn't have his teeth in, but Matt was too tired to laugh—or to argue with him. As he climbed, he fought the hiccups that always came after he cried.

Still breathing hard, Ray settled next to him. They dangled their feet over the side. Harvey handed up his flashlight and took Ray's shovel. They watched him clear the head of the coffin.

"This is 'cause you'll spend the rest of your life wonderin' what's what," Harvey said between shovelfuls. "I don't know if I'm doin' the right thing, so if you wake up in a few decades, nightmares hauntin' you, and you're cursin' my ghost, just remember, I did it for your own good. Sometimes not knowin' is worse 'n' knowin'."

Finally, he quit scooping dirt, took a long breath, and leaned down to pull the casket lid back. Matt aimed the flashlight inside. Ray gasped, but Matt just stared at the purple lining topped by a thin, lacy pillow.

The coffin was empty. He looked at Harvey, who had a peculiar expression on his face, and then back at the coffin. "She's not dead. I really did see my mom today."

Harvey climbed out of the grave and took the flashlight from Matt's hands. "Come with me."

They followed him to his trailer, neither boy speaking a word. Matt looked up at the stars. The moon had moved across the sky. He wondered what time it was.

The lights were on again in Harvey's trailer. So was the porch light, a welcome relief after the dark hole. Five stairs led to the door. At the base of the steps, Harvey said,

"Wipe your feet and brush the dirt off your clothes."

They did what they were told, then followed Harvey inside. He motioned to the couch and left the room but returned immediately. Matt thought he caught a glimpse of dentures between the old man's thin lips. Harvey lifted the receiver from a phone beside his easy chair and dialed a series of numbers. After several seconds, he said, "He knows."

Matt looked at Ray next to him on the couch.

Ray shrugged.

Harvey didn't speak for what felt like a long time. Finally, he said, "He's a bright kid. You shouldn't have..." He nodded, though the person on the other end couldn't see him. "All right."

He replaced the receiver.

"That the police?" Matt ran a sleeve over his face, wiping sweat from his eyes. "Am I going to jail?"

"No, you ain't goin' to jail." Harvey sighed. "We're goin' for a ride."

———————

Fifty miles and two farm towns later, Matt was roused from his travel stupor when Harvey slowed the truck to park in front of a hotel. He glanced at the caretaker, who looked even older in the artificial light.

Harvey motioned with his chin. "She's in there."

Matt's heart began to thump. What was his mother doing in a hotel? Was it really her? How did Harvey know where to find her? But he knew better than to ask. He'd tried to get answers earlier in the trip but had received no response to his questions.

He was about to awaken Ray, who was curled against

the passenger door, fast asleep, when Harvey said, "Let him be," and opened the driver-side door.

Heart racing, Matt stepped alone into the brightly lit hotel lobby. And there she was. His mother. She was wearing a pink robe and slippers he'd never seen before, and her hair was a different color. She looked tired and worried, but she was alive.

He frowned. He wanted to reject her, to hurt her like she'd hurt him.

She reached out her arms.

He cried, "Mom!" and ran to her.

"Matty." She held him close. "I've missed you so much."

"Why, Mom?" Matt sobbed. "Why'd you pretend to be dead?" He could barely say the words.

She led him to a couch and sat next to him. "Honey, there's something you need to know about your father."

"I don't care about Dad...he doesn't miss you. He likes Darla." Matt hiccupped and wiped his eyes. "But *I* miss you, Mom."

Conflicting emotions flickered across her face. "I know." She drew his head to her shoulder.

He closed his eyes and soaked up her presence, her sweet scent, her warmth. His mother was alive. "Mom, I don't want to go home."

"I don't want you to go."

He pulled away. "But what happened? Why did you...?"

She took his hands. "It's hard for me to tell you this, but you need to know. Arthur Wamer is a mean, violent man. When my friends realized my life was in danger, they helped me figure out a plan. Your father needed to think I was dead. That was the only way I could escape from

[154]

him." She looked deep into his eyes. "He threatened to kill me, Matty."

Matt shivered and, for the first time, noticed the television at the other end of the empty lobby. *The Star Spangled Banner* was playing and a picture of a flag filled the screen. While he watched, the last strains of the song faded to static and the screen turned white.

His mom slid a strand of hair off his forehead. "I'm so sorry for putting you through this. But your grief had to be real. Otherwise, Arthur might have suspected something."

He nodded. As awful as it was, her logic made sense.

"Harvey helped...and others. But they're sworn to secrecy."

"Ray knows. We saw your empty coffin."

She looked him over. "Is that why you're so dirty? You..." Tears brimmed in her eyes. "I would never have hurt you like this, if I could have thought of another way to protect us. I'll make it up to you."

"Please don't let Harvey take me back."

"Don't worry. He's not going to do that. We'll start a new life together, you and I." She smiled. "Arizona?"

Matt nodded. "Yeah, Arizona."

His mother motioned at the window and stood. Matt joined her. Seconds later, Harvey walked in with a barely awake Ray at his side.

Ray stared at Matt's mom. "You're really...?"

She smiled and explained how important it was for him to tell people his friend had disappeared during the night. If the police questioned him, he was to say Matt ran away to his grandparents' house.

She turned to her son. "We'd planned to spirit you

away after a few weeks and have you show up at my parents' place. They'll let us stay with them until we figure out our next step."

"What about Dad?"

She looked down, and he knew. His father wouldn't even miss him. He had Darla.

Ray swallowed. "If it means life and death, I'm tellin' nobody."

"Thanks, man." Matt slugged his friend's shoulder and leaned close. He lowered his voice. "There's a flat dime by the co-op, near the tracks. You can have it." Ray would know what he meant.

Ray rubbed his pant legs and looked at the carpet. "Thanks."

Harvey touched Matt's mother's arm. "I hate to see you go."

"You've been a huge help, Harvey." She stood on her tiptoes and gave the old man a big hug. "Without you, neither Matt nor I would be here. I can't begin to thank you enough." She dropped down, once again flatfooted in her slippers. "I'll miss you."

Harvey looked embarrassed. "Better head back. Gotta get the boy home and fill a hole before sunup." He rubbed Matt's head. "Take care of your mom."

Matt nodded.

Harvey put his hand on Ray's shoulder, and the two of them walked out the lobby door.

Matt looked up at his mother. "Did I make trouble for you, Mom?"

"Don't even think that for a minute." She put an arm around him. "I'm just thankful we're together again."

[156]

He sighed. "It was really hard seeing you today by the railroad tracks."

She turned to face him. "What do you mean?"

"When you ran from me and jumped in the car. That's how I knew you were alive."

"I wasn't by the tracks." She shook her head. "I don't dare return to that town. In fact, I've been in my room all day, waiting to hear from a contact who's arranging my—our—transportation to the next place."

Matt frowned. He was positive he'd seen her. And the tire marks…

"It doesn't matter." She pulled him close. "I'm just happy you're with me."

He wrapped his arms around her waist. His mom might never understand, but it *did* matter. What happened today at the railroad tracks mattered a great deal.

———————

INVISIBLE THREAD

Lisa Michelle Hess

Michael Johnson was about to take the stairs when a football wobbled to a stop at his feet. He recognized the two boys who were tossing the ball around. They lived in one of the condos down the street from his office. The nearest kid yelled at him, a rakish grin on his face, "Throw it back, mister."

Michael had talked several times with the boy, who wasn't old enough to be complicated. He was irrepressibly confident, and Michael liked that.

He set his coffee and briefcase down, picked up the ball, and ran his thumb along the threads. Feinting an underhand toss to the kid closest to him, he yelled, "Go long!" to his friend down the street, who backed up, running sideways. Michael launched the football in a perfect spiral, straight and true, right into the boy's outstretched hands. Both boys leaped into the air, shouting and jabbing their fists high above their heads.

Michael smiled. His training was useful in so many ways.

"Do it again," the boys yelled.

But Michael just waved, gathered his things and climbed the steps of the old brownstone that, like himself, was attractive but not too handsome and went unnoticed by most people. Even the name on the tarnished brass plaque next to the door, *Johnson and Associates Investments, LLP,* was not legible from the street. It could only be read from the top of the steps, where no one other than Michael had any reason to venture.

Balancing his coffee cup on his briefcase, he punched in the combination that he alone knew and pushed his way inside. Though he'd been gone for less than a week, the old building smelled musty. He set the briefcase and coffee on his desk and dropped into his chair with a sigh. Would it be today? Would he finally have the answer he'd been waiting for?

Travel and other obligations had kept him from reviewing the digital videos stacked neatly in the safe. Even before he was assigned to Alise and her grandmother, his superiors in the home office had determined this mission was probably pointless. They believed that even if the elderly woman once knew valuable information, she would have forgotten it by now. Compared to his other projects, the recordings were low priority; yet, he was addicted to the information they supplied.

Due to reasons he refused to examine too closely, he had yet to include The Grandmother's most recent revelations in his reports. After all, his handler probably didn't expect anything more, if he ever thought of The Grandmother at all.

For Michael, however, this project had assumed a life of its own. It seemed as if the data and images on the recordings, coupled with the stories Alise shared with him each night, were conspiring to make him more introspective about human relationships than he normally allowed himself to be. What was the invisible thread that connected certain hearts across years, miles, memories?

He twisted the thick gold band on the ring finger of his left hand. When he chose to marry Alise, the union had been approved at the highest levels. He'd told them marriage was his best chance at gaining The Grandmother's confidence and fulfilling his mission, and they'd believed him. He'd even convinced his handler, the closest thing he had to a friend, that marrying Alise was just part of the job. However, his superior had warned him such an attachment was risky. He needed to keep Alise at an emotional arm's length. That was ten years ago.

Michael sat back and massaged his temples. The prospect of finally completing this mission should have made him ecstatic. Instead, he felt as if his head was about to explode. He went across the hall to the bathroom and splashed cold water on his face. It didn't help.

He dried his face before he wandered back into his office, where his hulking, black-metal floor safe loomed in the corner, a secure repository for the tapes. He would leave them there, like he did most days. His wife kept him up to date on the story her grandmother, Elaine, was slowly revealing, and he learned much more through Alise's retelling of the narrative than by viewing the videos. She was able to read between the lines of Elaine's story in a way that he, with all his skill, could not.

Michael paced the floor. Even with his wife's unwitting assistance, he still wasn't able to put all the pieces of The

Grandmother's past together. He plopped onto his leather couch and watched dust motes float in the ray of sunshine that streamed through the high window.

Closing his eyes, he calmed his breathing and focused on the facts he'd pieced together from previous operatives' reports, a handful of old letters, the daily recordings, and the few details Elaine had revealed over the years. He'd mulled over this same body of evidence many times before. But lately, he'd begun to feel as if his life depended on solving the mystery of her childhood years.

From what he knew, The Grandmother was born on September 15, 1910, in Crow Wing County, Minnesota. Her birth certificate christened her simply "Dickenson, female," as anyone with an Ancestry.com membership could discover. Her mother was twenty-years old. Her father, a mining engineer, was forty. Elaine believed they were married at the time.

By 1915, her parents had separated, and her father, Howard, had spirited her away to a gold mining camp in Sacramento, California. He called her Beatrice Viola and taught her to fold his clothes, to shape her letters, and that fire was hot and could burn. Old pictures and correspondence left no doubt she was precocious and beautiful. She was the apple of his eye, and he was the hero of her life. When Elaine spoke of her father, a smile played on her lips, like he was a secret only she knew, even as she revealed everything she could remember about him. At least, she said it was all she remembered.

In 1917, they sailed from San Francisco to Japan on the steamer *Victoria*. Elaine was the only child on the ship—and most of the men aboard wore uniforms. The bored sailors played with her and taught her a rhyme.

Kaiser Bill went up the hill to take a look at France.

Kaiser Bill went down the hill with bullets in his pants.

They traveled to Yokohama, Japan, then to Vladivostok, Russia. From there, they made their way by train to Chita, Russia. Known as the City of Exiles, Chita was perched on the Eastern edge of the maelstrom that was, to the United States, "the war to end all wars." For the Russians, it was a confusing swirl of Whites and Reds and shades of November gray, which, when the conflict finally settled, changed that country and the world forever.

But Elaine was only seven-years old when they arrived in Russia. How could she remember anything but snow and horse-drawn sleighs and a handsome, dashing father who told her everything would be all right and wasn't this a marvelous adventure?

By 1918, her father was dead, and she was living in Seattle with her Grandmother Ione, a fine-work dressmaker for wealthy women. Ione called her Elaine Beatrice. "Elaine" stuck, but Beatrice was dropped and forgotten—until recently.

Elaine Beatrice Dickenson Alden was one-hundred-and-two-years old, code named The Grandmother. Every day, she told Alise one new detail about her life as a child, putting flesh on the bare bones of the facts in his file, moving closer and closer to the answer he was waiting for. Why now, after all this time, was she finally filling in the blanks?

"Because, dear," she'd told Alise with a piercing look, "next year I won't remember anymore."

Michael checked his watch. His wife should be arriving at Elaine's any minute, and he didn't have the patience to wait, not today. He moved to his chair and switched on what looked like an investment consultant's computer. However, when the large screen came to life, he could see the interior of each room in Elaine's house. He focused on the stairwell leading to her bedroom.

Alise ran up the short flight of stairs, deftly skirting the electric elevator chair attached to the wall, and stopped at the doorway to her grandmother's bedroom. As she often did, Alise took time to study Elaine, who was perched on the bed's edge, clad in pajama bottoms and naked from the waist up, her back to the door.

By this point, his wife was familiar with every curve and wrinkle of her grandmother's ravaged-by-life body, and Michael tried to see Elaine through Alise's eyes. The smallpox had left scars, the children had left stretch marks. She'd lost one breast to cancer when she was in her sixties and the other to its return twenty years later.

Yet, as her grandmother straightened and stretched like a cat, Michael watched Alise smile. According to her, Elaine's beauty was timeless, classic. Based on the photos he'd seen, she'd always had a certain grace about her. The pictures left no doubt she'd once been quite beautiful, like a darker-haired twin to his fair, blond wife.

He glanced at the tray beside The Grandmother's bed, where her current life was scattered. He'd visited her enough to have the tray's contents memorized—hearing aid, eyeglasses, dishes from her evening snack, a half-full tumbler of water, books and magazines, and remote controls for the television and the DVD player. He could almost smell the scent in the room—something like burnt grass and oranges, and it made him smile. The Grandmother refused to "smell like an old person," and if she couldn't accomplish her goal through sheer force of will, she would use fire and pungent incense.

"Good morning, Gram." Alise's voice was raised as she crossed the room to the window and opened the curtains. "How are you this beautiful day?"

Without the hearing aid and glasses, Elaine didn't seem to notice Alise until sunlight spilled into the room. She lifted her gaze from the blouse Alise had left folded on the end of the bed the night before. Her eyes, normally so sharp, squinted—a bewildered look.

Michael clenched his fist. Was senility setting in? If so, she might never reveal the secrets he'd waited ten years to learn. After a few tense seconds, he was relieved to see Elaine's pursed mouth curve into a delighted smile. She cleared her throat. "There's my happy girl...I'm fine today. Just...slow."

Alise nodded with a sympathetic smile. Walking into Elaine's room, her world, was like stepping into a time-warp. Something as simple as writing a letter was scheduled a day in advance and only accomplished with dogged persistence. Getting to the bathroom and back was a major strategic accomplishment. This was the first time Michael had heard Elaine acknowledge her challenges, though, the closest she'd come to a complaint. Alise said her grandmother's courageous spirit was the reason she was so easy to care for, despite the crazy, childish whims that came with old age.

———————

Michael asked, "How was she today?"

Alise drew a breath and released it. She'd been distracted all evening. He guessed she was still a little lost in the world her grandmother had created with her story during their daily visit. "Slow," she finally responded, as if she'd just heard an echo of his words.

He let a beat pass. "Slow...how?"

She pressed her lips together.

Michael watched his wife mentally remind herself for the millionth time that this was the reason she fell in love with him. He was the only man she'd ever met who actually wanted to know what was going on in her head. She'd told him this.

Over the course of their marriage, however, she'd become less willing to share her thoughts, as if she expected him to read her mind. The irony... Still, he was obsessed with her inner world, and he would expose it word by begrudging word if he had to.

He smiled as she literally shrugged off her irritation. *Because she still loves me. Because she knows how many women would kill for a husband who actually listens.*

Alise refreshed her lemonade from the pitcher on the table in front of them, took a long swallow and closed her eyes for a moment, remembering. Michael recalled Elaine doing the very same thing earlier in the day, when his wife sat down beside her after breakfast. Alise sighed, opened her eyes, and proceeded to tell him her version of the latest installment in her grandmother's story.

They'd arrived at the Keystone Hotel in San Francisco sometime in the spring of 1917. The corporate bustle of the town was impressive after the rough-and-tumble mining camps from which they'd come. The streets were wide and the buildings tall.

To Beatrice, everyone appeared to be dressed in their Sunday best. She was too little to comprehend how travel-worn and poor she and her father looked in comparison as they left the train from Sacramento and made their way past the shops and businesses that lined Fourth Street. But Howard was apparently aware.

Before finding the Keystone, they stopped at one of the shops along the way and were fitted for a full wardrobe of fine clothing. The fabrics—velvets, satins, laces and linens that felt as soft as water against her skin—were more beautiful than anything Beatrice had ever imagined, and she had quite an imagination. Had they suddenly become wealthy, she wondered? But they must have—for everyone, after a few words of commerce with her tall, handsome papa, seemed eager to serve them.

When all the fittings were finished and orders given, they continued on through the crowded streets. Her father protected her as best he could, yet she was occasionally bumped and jostled by drunken sailors, self-important businessmen, and women dressed in garish finery. It didn't bother her, much. She knew Papa would keep her safe, and besides, she was just like him, always ready for adventure. Howard said it often, and Beatrice agreed—anything was better than boredom.

Finally, they stepped through tall double doors into the quiet coolness of the Keystone. It took time to adjust to the dim lighting. Beatrice closed her eyes and relished the feeling of uncrowded space and the comforting smells of floor wax and furniture polish—the scents of her grandmother's house. Her remembrance of home was almost a sob, but then she opened her eyes and all thoughts of her past were forgotten.

A white marble floor stretched before her like a sheet of ice, reminding her of twilight on a perfect winter day, while sparkling crystals dripped from the chandeliers hanging high above her head. Snowy white plaster molding frothed at the tops of walls and spread across the ceiling. In contrast, ebony-scrolled metal railing accompanied the stairs to the upper rooms.

Deep-brown mahogany edged the marble floor, rose in wainscoting halfway up the white walls, and covered the front of the curved registration desk where her father led her. The wood was polished to such a sheen she could see her reflection. She admired herself in her new dress while her father conversed with the man behind the tall desk. When she grew bored, she stood on her tiptoes, but she couldn't see over the top.

The bellman was finally called. He took their bags and led them to an elegant two-bedroom suite on the second floor. Beatrice wandered slowly through their new quarters, touching the green velvet-backed chairs, smiling at the gilded mirrors. The suite had a sitting room and was cleaner than any place she'd inhabited for years.

Not many days later, a woman named Dani joined them in their suite. She was Irish-Indian and had been raised in India. Her copper-colored skin was accented by long, silky, black hair, and she spoke with a soft, musical accent Beatrice loved. Howard told everyone Dani was Beatrice's nurse, and indeed Dani was very nurturing.

She taught Beatrice how to read, how to wear the beautiful clothing that was delivered to them, and what was appropriate and inappropriate behavior when dining with the many society people who met with her father. Beatrice, little as she was, understood there was a fondness between Howard and Dani that went well beyond a business relationship. She also somehow knew she wasn't to question it.

One day, Howard entered their suite earlier than usual. His brow was furrowed and he appeared to be lost in contemplation, as if he barely noticed he'd entered the room. But then he blinked, looked up and seemed to become aware of his surroundings. To the little girl's relief, his solemn expression quickly transformed into the mock seriousness he used when he was discussing her studies and deportment.

"And how is the child today, Dani?"

Dani smiled. "Howard, you know she is lovely, a pleasure to teach. I have never seen a child learn so quickly."

In a few strides of his long legs, he was across the room and swinging Beatrice into the air, to the delighted shrieks of the child. "Well, of course." He laughed. "She's a Dickenson, is she not?"

Their indulgence didn't spoil her. She basked and grew in the pleasure they took in her, like the petals of a flower reaching out to morning sun.

Later that night, as Beatrice lay in her bed listening to Howard and Dani talk in the sitting room, she heard for the first time the name of the ship they would sail on—The Victoria.

"There's a group of railroad men we'll meet in Yokohama, and we'll continue on to Vladivostok with them," Howard said. "They'll look like regular army down to the uniforms and all, but William says not. They're attached to the state department."

"Why on earth are they sending them on the mission?"

"Ostensibly to help the Russians modernize their system, but William thinks it's mainly to ensure the supplies the U.S. has stocked in Vladivostok and the other rail stations along the Trans-Siberian Railway don't fall into German hands, if the Russians make peace with them—and it looks like they might."

Dani sighed. "I can't keep track of what country is doing

what. It's all such a mess."

"It is that," Howard agreed.

After a time, Dani asked, "Are you sure it's safe? What about Beatrice?"

"It's perfectly safe, Dani. Do you think I'd risk the well-being of either one of you?" Howard's voice took on its usual confident tone, which relieved Beatrice. She didn't like the fear and uncertainty she heard in Dani's voice.

She focused on Papa's voice instead. "It's business as usual for American corporations," he said, "and diplomats in Yokohama, Vladivostok and Petrograd. Our proposed route is the same one we'd hoped to follow, after all. My part will be nothing but a babysitting mission for a few days. I'll ensure the package gets on the train and then off again and into the right hands. Then we'll be done and can continue on as we planned."

His voice took on a tender note. "Really, darling, there's nothing to fear. I think we're the only people the Russians trust right now. They certainly don't trust the British or the Germans."

"With good reason, Howard." Dani sounded angry. "Their trust will be the least we have to lose if they find out what you're up to."

Alise stopped, and Michael asked, although he already knew the answer, "What was he up to?"

She laughed and rose to clear away the dishes. "I have no idea. That's where she ended the story. You know, it's almost like she's reluctant to tell me."

"Maybe you shouldn't pressure her."

"What do you mean?" Alise frowned. "I'm not

pressuring her."

What was he doing? He held up a hand, smoothly covering his confusion. "I just mean, Russia has to be a bad memory for her. Her father died there, right? And she nearly died, as well."

She shook her head. "I think she likes to talk about her adventures. You know Gram. She wouldn't have brought up the subject if it was a bad memory. *Accentuate the Positive* is one of her favorite songs." Alise shrugged and reached for his plate. "I do sense she's reluctant to talk about parts of the story, though. It's almost like she's waiting for something."

———————

Alise helped Elaine to the bathroom and back, settled her into the double recliner where she spent most of the day, and prepared a tray with the hot tea and bran muffin she'd requested for her afternoon snack. She watered Elaine's prized violets on the dresser, vacuumed the floor, changed the sheets on her bed, and finished with a plumping of the pillows.

Elaine motioned to her with an incense stick. "Lie down on the bed and take a load off, dear." She lit the stick with a flourish. "A woman should put her feet up for thirty minutes in the middle of every day."

Alise smiled. "You read that in a Better Homes and Gardens in 1959."

"Oh, no, Alise." Elaine looked serious. "That's wisdom direct from your Great-Grandmother Ione. No matter how busy I was, I took the time every day of my life to follow her advice."

Alise held up her hand. "I know what you're going to

say next. Midday rests are the reason you've lived this many years." She chuckled. "I say you've lived this long because you're so stubborn." But she climbed onto the bed and leaned back against the high pillows with a sigh.

Through the window above the bed, Michael could see trees swaying in a breeze. Fall light and shadows rippled across his wife's motionless form. Alise was pretty, but in a different way than Elaine. The Grandmother, with her slightly slanted eyes that were still a shocking sapphire blue, had an exotic look about her. In her younger years, her long, shiny hair had been almost black. She'd had a full bosom and a tiny waist —and dressed to accentuate both.

In contrast, Alise was petite, athletic and fair. She rarely gave a thought to what she wore or how she looked. When the two were together, however, the fact they were related was unmistakable. They had the same eyes and nose, the same full lips. But more than that, the way they carried themselves was similar.

They were both relaxed yet self-possessed and utterly in control. Women who were never hurried, yet always on time, they inspired in people an undeniable desire to please them. The main difference between the two was that, while Elaine was quite conscious of her power, Alise seemed unaware of the spell she cast on those around her.

"Now, where was I?" Elaine asked.

"You were telling me about Grandpa Tobias."

"Ah, yes. He was the most handsome man I'd seen since I lost Papa." Elaine smiled. "So kind...and so intelligent. He barely had an eighth-grade education, but he was always reading and learning, and he had a sixth sense about the next thing like I've never seen."

Michael knew Tobias's history as well as he knew The

Grandmother's. The man's ancestral roots went back to colonial days, and his Puritan work ethic had equaled Elaine's drive. They'd made an unbeatable entrepreneurial team, developing businesses and selling products together for sixty years. Eventually, they retired to a cozy two-story on a wooded street.

"My only quarrel with your grandfather," Elaine said, "was that he hated to travel. The farthest I could get him to go was the shortest route possible to the ocean, two or three times a year." She shook her head. "He was a homebody, for sure, which chafed at me, for a while. But then, he was such *fine* company. Tobias was always thinking about something new to make, or to buy, or to sell. *He* became my adventure."

"Do you think Grandpa reminded you of your father?" Alise asked. "Is that partly what made you fall in love with him?"

Elaine was quiet. Finally, she nodded. "Perhaps...yes, perhaps. Although, of course, Papa loved to travel. He was an engineer, and he'd worked repairing diamond drill bits for gold mines all over the world before I was born. He just happened to meet my mother one day when he was home visiting his parents. He'd been working in the wild northland, Alaska, and before that, Africa. He was in his forties when I was born, which was why he was too old for the draft when the U.S. entered the war in 1917. However, he was already in government service."

Michael leaned closer to the monitor. She'd made the comment almost as an afterthought—and it took Alise a moment to catch the implication. "Government service? How? I thought your trip to Russia had to do with selling mining and drilling equipment."

"Well..." Elaine seemed to be choosing her words

carefully. "Yes...at first, and selling equipment to the Russians continued to be the reason he gave for the trip."

"Gram..." Alise sat up and turned to Elaine. "You're killing me. *Why* did you go to Russia in 1917? Did it have to do with the war?"

Michael reached for the phone. Was The Grandmother about to say the words he'd waited ten years to hear? Then why this nearly undeniable urge to interrupt the conversation before she changed their lives forever? He sat back, shaking his head. Was he losing his mind? Besides, Alise was right. Elaine was a stubborn woman who would eventually say what she wanted to say.

He watched her consider her granddaughter across the room. "Oh, Alise, do you really want to know? That's ancient history. What does it matter now?"

"Learning about your past is important to me." Alise got up from the bed and sat next to her grandmother on the recliner. "And sharing your life story obviously matters to you. Gram, I *really* want to know."

"All right," Elaine smiled approvingly, as if Alise had passed some test. "I'll tell you. But first, you have to answer a question of mine. It's one I've had on my mind for quite some time."

"Of course, anything."

"I don't like to mess about in things that aren't my business, and I'll admit this is none of my business. But, Alise, only the two of us are left of our family. I've often wondered why you haven't any children."

Michael folded his arms and waited to hear her response.

Alise's smile faded. She opened her mouth, then closed it.

Elaine squeezed her hand. "I don't mean to pry, but it's not that you can't have them, is it?"

His wife slowly shook her head. "I can have children. At least, I've no reason to think I can't."

"Well, then, what is it? Don't you want them? I've heard all kinds of women in their forties are having children these days."

Alise's gaze moved to the window, as if she was trying to make out something in the distance. "I don't really know. I wanted kids when I was younger, before Dad was killed and Mom got sick." She shrugged. "I always pictured Mom enjoying them with me, helping me bring them up. Instead, I ended up taking care of her and…"

"And that was enough." Elaine nodded. "And now you're taking care of me."

Alise knelt beside Elaine and looked up into her eyes. "Gram, you know I love to spend time with you. I'd be here every day, even if you didn't need my help."

Elaine chuckled. "That's probably true. But you still haven't answered my question."

Like a child, Alise laid her head on her grandmother's lap, and Elaine rested her hand on her red-gold curls. "That's because I don't know the answer," Alise said. "I mean, look at the world. Is it really fair to bring a child into it? And Michael travels so much, I'd practically be a single mother."

"Trust me, the world's no worse than it's ever been." Elaine lifted her granddaughter's chin with a finger. "I know what you've suffered. But you mustn't let your father's accident and your mother's illness color your world. Death is a part of life, and children accept that easier than adults."

Alise sat beside Elaine again. "Is it really that easy? Was it for you?"

"Well," Elaine allowed, "not easy. But simple. We're the ones who complicate it. Besides, you'll create your children's world. It's all in how you teach them to see it. You teach them to focus on the good and not the bad...and then as they get older, to make the bad and the good better, as the opportunity arises."

"Is that what you did?"

Elaine patted Alise's hand. "You know it is, and how your mother taught you as well. And that's how you'll teach your own children."

"But Michael..."

"Does he not want children?"

Alise looked away. "We've never talked about children."

Michael groaned, remembering the handful of times she'd brought up the subject and he'd immediately distracted her. But that was before—

"You've never discussed it? Even before you married?" Elaine sounded shocked.

Alise raised her chin, defensive. "Well, of course, in a general kind of way. But never in any definite way, like some people do."

Elaine appeared stricken by the information. "That's so odd," she said, as if to herself. "I thought you told him everything."

"He's happy the way we are, I suppose. At least he never mentions children."

Michael was surprised by the longing in her voice. He hadn't realized...

"And you, Alise? Are you happy? What if Michael wasn't traveling so much? He won't always travel, will he? Would you think about starting a family then?"

"Oh, I think about it, Gram. I think about it all the time." She smiled and gave her grandmother a wink. "Now, I've answered your question. Your turn."

Elaine gave Alise a searching look. "Well, all right. But, let's see... First, I have to back up. How much do you know about The War? Do they even teach children about it in school any longer? These days, I suppose it's all Vietnam, and Iraq and Afghanistan."

Alise laughed. "I'm ashamed to admit, Gram, I don't know much about World War One. That war was over almost before it began for the U.S., wasn't it?"

"The first world war..." Elaine rubbed her forehead. "Well, like Dani said, it was a mess. A huge, reeking mess that twisted the world, then hung it out to dry. And, my dear, the world hasn't been the same since."

————

Though the call came at nine o'clock a.m. London time, it kept Michael at the office past midnight. He expected Alise to be asleep by the time he arrived home. Yet, light spilled through the partially opened bedroom door. He moved closer, slowly, quietly, and peeked in.

Dressed in one of his t-shirts, she sat on the floor surrounded by pictures and mementos from one of the many bins of family archives she stored under the bed. Black tights hugged her legs. Wisps of red-gold escaped her headband and coiled in tendrils around her face.

He could smell her vanilla-almond lotion from the doorway. As always, the warm, sweet scent awakened his longing, as did the roundness of her breasts beneath his shirt, the stray ringlets just brushing the line of her jaw, and the way the tights hugged her athletic legs like a second skin. Every part of him responded to every part of her so strongly it verged on pain. This was one of the few facts about himself he'd never hidden from her.

She didn't believe him. Whenever he mentioned how beautiful he found her, she laughed it off like he'd just delivered an embarrassing pickup line. She didn't understand the hold she had on him, and that was good.

Alise was aware of him watching her, though. He was a professional, yet sneaking up on his wife was nearly impossible. She lifted those blue eyes to his and smiled. "Well, look who finally decided to come home."

His heart skipped a beat, but he just said, "London conference call," and moved past her toward the closet, removing his jacket as he went. "You're up late."

"Way too late." She gestured at the mess around her. "I was trying to find a letter Gram gave me for the archives years ago. She said it was the last letter her father wrote before he died. She talked about it today."

He responded from the depths of the walk-in closet. "Did you find it?"

"Yes. I knew right where it was. But then I start looking at this stuff, these pictures, and I can't stop. Look, Michael, do you remember this?" He poked his head out, and she held up an old photograph, one he'd shot the day they met. All the pictures in the bin were at least a decade old. Newer ones were digital. They went onto a compact disk and were never seen again.

He loosened his tie and stooped to kiss her upturned lips. Tempted to fulfill his earlier fantasy, he lingered. But then he remembered the picture and the possibility his wife might have a new revelation for him.

"Help me stand, Michael. I've been sitting cross-legged for too long."

He helped her to her feet, kissed her again, and took the picture from her. This one, snapped a few days after he arrived in town, was nearly twenty years old and beginning to fade. In it, Alise and The Grandmother sat on a park bench surrounded by squirrels and pigeons. He'd never forgotten that day, which also happened to be Alise's birthday.

Elaine had hired a nurse for the day to care for her daughter, Alise's mother, who was slowly wasting away from a mysterious brain disease. Elaine had treated Alise to lunch and then they'd walked in the park. To Michael's dismay, the older woman caught sight of him watching with his camera and gestured him over. "Take our picture, young man," she'd commanded. "We never get a picture with both of us in it."

Alise looked pale and tired in the photo. But she was smiling happily at the camera, at him. The look on Elaine's face was harder to read.

Looking at the picture, Michael realized he'd tripped into trouble the first time he saw Alise smile. Most people faked their way through life, pretending to be something they were not, hiding their true feelings, their true values and priorities. Those people were simple for Michael to read. He'd been trained to discover their secrets, and he did so easily.

He also found them boring. But when Alise smiled that day, he'd been blown away. It was all there in her eyes—the tragedy she lived through each day with her mother as well as, inexplicably, hope and joy. Her truth was written across her face and in every beautiful move she made, and she didn't care who knew it. Honesty, like Alise, always surprised him.

Somehow, he'd ended up spending the afternoon with the two of them. And, of course, he had to see Alise again to give her the picture. The rest was, as they say, history. He still felt a little guilty about his good fortune and how they'd so easily let him in to their simple love. He'd been able to spend all these years as a part of their family.

He knew he was taking advantage of them. But he didn't take them for granted. He'd done his best to honor and care for both of them.

"Of course I remember that day." He put his arm around her. "And I remember you apologized for feeding the squirrels right next to the *No Feeding the Wildlife* sign. 'But she's eighty years old,' you said, 'and if she wants to feed the squirrels, then she gets to feed the squirrels.'"

Alise smiled.

He knew she knew what he was going to say next, but he continued anyway. "If I'd known then the number of times I would to hear *that* excuse..." He switched to a high voice to mimic hers. "She's ninety-two years old. If she wants me to make Bavarian cream pie from scratch for her birthday, then I'll figure out how to make Bavarian cream pie. She's ninety-six years old and never goes anywhere, but if she wants red patent leather sandals, then I'm buying her red patent leather sandals."

Alise laughed and pushed him onto the bed. "Oh, stop! You know you love her, too." She flopped on top of him, but he rolled the two of them over. "I know I love you," he said, and for the rest of the evening, he didn't care if she had a thought in her head.

———————

"Alise?" he said much later as they lay on the bed, having untangled themselves.

"Hmmm?" she responded drowsily.

"What was the letter you were looking for?"

"Oh, just something she wanted me to take to her tomorrow. Something to do with her father." Alise opened her eyes and turned toward him. "She told me the most amazing story today."

"About what?" They must have picked up the conversation later, when he left the office to run an errand across town.

She turned her back to Michael and slipped into the curve of his body. "About why they were in Russia in 1917."

He blinked, now wide awake, but continued to breathe slowly, evenly. He was trained for this. "Really?" He kept his voice neutral but interested. "Why were they there?"

"Oh..." She was falling back to sleep. "It's too long to tell you now." She yawned. "I'll tell you tomorrow."

After a minute, he said, "Alise?" But she was asleep.

———————

His wife stood ten feet away, a pink-blanketed bundle in her arms. She smiled her beautiful, playful smile and, without any warning, tossed the bundle toward him.

Michael shouted, "No!" and held out his hands. Against all odds, he caught the child, his child, and exhaled in relief. Once again, his training had come through for him. But when he looked down, he didn't see a baby in his arms. He saw a football.

Alise chuckled. "Throw it back, Michael. Throw it back."

———————

He awoke with a start. Morning sun poured into their bedroom window, illuminating a still-sleeping Alise next to him. He climbed out of bed without waking her, pulled on some sweats and headed for the kitchen. He knew the smell of fresh-ground coffee brewing would lure her from the bedroom, and it worked.

Bleary-eyed, she materialized in the kitchen just as the coffee was ready. Alise picked up her mug from the counter and held it out to him. He kissed her cheek before pouring her a full cup. She grunted and stumbled to the sofa, where she curled against the armrest, all the while clutching the huge cup with both hands. Once settled, she raised it to her lips.

Michael tossed the *Wall Street Journal* he'd been reading onto the coffee table and sat in the easy chair across from her, mug in hand.

She gave him a dirty look. "You kept me awake until two a.m."

He lifted an eyebrow. "You're the one who waited up for me in that sexy outfit."

"Yeah." She snorted. "Real sexy."

"If only you knew." He drank some coffee. "Just thinking about it makes me want to—"

She lifted a hand. "Don't go there, Michael. I need to shower and head over to help Grandmother."

"On top of that, you started a story and then promptly fell asleep."

Alise cocked her head. "What story?"

"Something about Elaine's father and why they went to Russia."

"Oh, yeah." Her gaze moved to the window, and she took another sip of coffee.

"So, spill it," he said casually, as if The Grandmother's story was barely more interesting to him than the newspaper he'd been reading.

She gave him a resentful look that clearly said he was greedy beyond words for wanting even more of her than she'd given him the night before. But he could be merciless—how merciless, she had no idea—and patient.

Finally, she put her coffee down, stretched her legs out on the coffee table, crossed them, and began the part of the story he hadn't yet viewed.

———————

"It was really just a war between men trying to build empires," Elaine had said. "Political ones and financial ones. But the world had become too small for the empire builders, and they'd started to stumble over each other."

At that, she'd shaken her head in disgust. "The British and French only cared about the Russians insofar as they were keeping a substantial portion of the German army busy on the Eastern Front. If the Russians stopped fighting, the Germans would move their troops to the Western Front, which was territory the Allies were just barely defending.

"They didn't give a fig for what was happening to the Russian people, or the fact the Bolsheviks had seized power and assassinated the royal family. The Allies were content to let them continue their little Marxist experiment because they didn't believe it would last long. From a political standpoint, they thought of the situation as similar to children taking over a playroom. They would have been content to wait until it all devolved into anarchy. So what if the Russian people were starving to death."

Elaine took a minute to catch her breath and drink some tea. The subject seemed to have given her new energy.

"But the Bolsheviks were threatening peace with the Germans—they'd gotten into power by promising to extricate Russia from the war—and then they actually started to negotiate with the Germans. Well..." Elaine chuckled. "This was a nightmare scenario for the Allies, especially the British. So they hit upon a plan.

"They decided there was no negotiating with the Bolsheviks, although they continued to pretend diplomacy, and determined the only option to change the situation to their advantage was through covert means. Money was to be their savior. They found a conservative Russian financier who already owned substantial interests in a number of Russia's largest banks. He offered to help the British appropriate the major banks in Russia and give the Allies controlling seats on the boards." Elaine stopped. "Do you see what they were doing, Alise?"

Her granddaughter nodded. "They would own...well, Russia's economy, wouldn't they?"

"Exactly," Elaine said. "No Russian government would be able to function without their say-so. If it had worked, the scheme would have turned the Russian Empire into just another colony of the British Empire."

"But how does all this relate to you and your father?

This was the British, right? What did Howard have to do with it? I mean, was the U.S. even in the war yet?"

"Just barely," Elaine said. "But they weren't anywhere near the Eastern Front, and they certainly hadn't declared war on Russia, which was why what happened next took place in the utmost secrecy. There were many flaws in the plan, the biggest being the Russian financier needed a huge loan in order to buy out the current board members. The value of the ruble was plummeting like a shooting star, and the board members in question wanted British pounds so they could flee the country. Unfortunately, the British, after four years of war, didn't have the extra cash to spend on taking over a country. They needed a loan, too, and who do you think they went to for financing?"

"The United States," Alise responded, eyes wide.

"Right, and the U.S. was more than willing to comply. But, of course, the Americans demanded some guarantee their money would be put to good use. The British say the Russian, who was in Siberia at the time, guaranteed the loan with hundreds of thousands of rubles he sent with a messenger to the British Embassy in Petrograd. But the messenger never arrived, or so the story goes. The problem with that account is, as I said, no one would have accepted rubles as a guarantee against anything at that point.

"None of that mattered, anyway," Elaine said with a wave of her hand. "What they all underestimated was the depth of weariness and disgust the Russian people had concerning the war. They would have handed over their country to the devil himself, if he'd promised to get them out of the conflict. The Bolsheviks were the only ones who told them what they wanted to hear, so it wasn't long before the Bolsheviks simply nationalized all the banks,

Trotsky's army defeated their Cossack enemies in the South, and the Allies fled Petrograd."

"Amazing," Alise said. "But I still don't understand what this has to do with you."

Elaine shrugged. "Well, of course, I didn't understand any of this as a child. It was all just a grand adventure. I was the only child on board that huge ship and had the run of the place. The younger sailors were my playmates. They spoiled me rotten, taught me deplorable language and gave me candy when Dani wasn't looking." She smiled at the memory.

"One grand old British dame sailed with us. I don't know who she was, and I've never been able to locate the ship's manifest. But I remember her implying at dinner one night that it was an error for Papa to bring me along on the trip across the ocean.

"Why don't you simply send her to a convent?" the woman asked, as direct and imperious as she always was whenever they encountered her. Like most adults, she seemed to believe small children didn't hear what adults said, and if they did hear, they didn't understand.

"Perhaps I should," Howard said, as if taking her seriously. Under the table, he gave the little girl's hand a squeeze. "But then, get along without my Beatrice? No, that would never do. She's my guardian angel, madam." And it was the way he said 'madam,' very polite but with a steely edge to his voice, that sent a shiver through Beatrice. The woman never brought up the subject again.

In Yokohama, Beatrice and Dani spent their days exploring the city via rickshaw and the surrounding countryside by train. The war seemed very far away. Their hotel was teeming with foreigners—mostly American and British businessmen and diplomats going about their business, just as Howard had said. One day, Howard came back to the hotel and announced they must pack their things. They would leave the next day.

"The Bolsheviks have decided to allow the railway men in, after all," he announced to Dani, rubbing his hands together. "We'll be sailing with them in the morning. Then it's just a matter of meeting up with our contact in Chita, picking up the rest of the equipment in Novo Nikolaevsk, and completing our business."

Dani seemed much less enthusiastic than Beatrice's father. "They're going ahead with the plan? Really? I've heard negotiations have broken down with the Germans, that the German forces are making their way toward Petrograd..." She looked nervously toward Beatrice and then back at Howard. "I've heard there is quite a bit of...unrest...in the country," she finished softly.

"Dani, you worry too much," Howard said. "I've told them I won't go all the way to Petrograd, just to be sure we don't get in the middle of that mess. We'll be handing the package off at Novo-Nikolaevsk and then heading back. It'll be fine. The two of you can even stay in Chita until I return, if you'd like."

"I think that might be best," Dani said, and she sounded relieved.

They arrived in Vladivostok in the dead of winter and immediately boarded a train headed northwest toward Chita and the edge of the Siberian frontier. To Beatrice, it was as if the war began while their train traveled from Vladivostok to their first stop on the Trans-Siberian Railway. They stepped off the train to stretch their legs and had to move aside quickly as uniformed Russian soldiers surged around them to board the train.

Wounded and sick men lay or sat in clusters on the crowded platform. Some on stretchers were attended by Red Cross workers. The noise of war was shocking to her young ears. Wounded men groaned and cried. Uniformed soldiers shouted orders. Workers frantically loaded and unloaded cargo, which banged and crashed onto the platform near them. The air smelled salty and sour—sweat mingled with refuse and blood.

Beatrice felt Dani's hand tighten on hers, and Howard quickly bundled them back onto the train. He promised they would spend more time walking around at the next stop. But every stop was the same. More and more soldiers boarded the train, until it was standing room only. Every station was filled with sick and wounded men and reverberated with cacophony and chaos.

Seated safely between Dani and Howard, Beatrice heard snatches of their whispered words intermixed with snippets of other passengers' conversations.

"Howard, has the entire world come to Russia to fight?" Dani asked. "So many different uniforms. I've heard Japanese, Chinese, French and Italian spoken, as well as English and Russian. What is everyone doing here?"

"No one seems to know." Howard leaned over Beatrice to murmur in Dani's ear. "I talked with one of the railway men on the ship. They don't know why they've been sent over, other than their presence is important to the American government."

He shook his head. "The Germans are advancing toward Petrograd, and I'm afraid this country is falling apart. Influenza and smallpox are on the rise, too, they say. All this happened while we were aboard ship. If I'd known..."

Beatrice couldn't hear the rest, but she could tell they were both worried.

Even so, Howard joked and laughed with the soldiers and exchanged cigarettes for information and drinks from flasks they were passing between them. And he never forgot Beatrice. Once, he pointed out the window at the pink-and-orange sunset that glowed above the mountains. "Look how beautiful the sky is, Bea."

He smiled warmly, kissed her forehead and hugged her close. She could feel the tension in the two bodies that flanked her, though, and sensed Russia was not a safe place. At some point during the long train ride, she started to lose focus. By the time they reached their destination, she'd begun to feel alternately sluggish and then dizzily light. The rest of the trip seemed to take the form of a waking dream.

They arrived in Chita at night. Dani helped Beatrice bundle into the fur-lined hat, muffler and boots they'd purchased for her in Vladivostok. After she was lifted into a wagon, warm blankets were tucked around her. Then the driver shook the reins and the wagon started with a lurch. Encircled in Dani's arms, Beatrice remembered nothing more of the journey from the railway station.

The next morning, she awoke to gray light coming through the window above her and the sound of children's laughter in the distance. Wrapped in thick blankets, she was lying on a pallet in the corner of a large room. A woman she didn't recognize was stirring a pot over a fire in the center, and her father and Dani were seated at a nearby table.

Howard was speaking. "I'm to meet my contact at a mine a few hours ride from here." He took a bite of what might have been porridge and then continued. "The gold will be packed in crates that look like they contain drill bits. I'll have those delivered directly to the train station and get passage as soon as I can to Nikolaevsk, where I'll exchange the crates for the real parts and accompany them back here. We'll do our business and then head straight for America, I promise."

"I don't like this, Howard." Dani grabbed his arm. "If we wait too long, we may not get out until the war is over. And I'm worried about Beatrice. She isn't well...and you're not looking any too healthy yourself."

For a time, there were only the sounds of the woman tending to the fire, the children playing outside, and Dani and her father eating. Beatrice watched as lacy snowflakes landed on the window and slowly slid down, piling into a slushy hill at the bottom.

"I'm just tired," Howard finally said. "I'm concerned about Beatrice, too. But if she's sick, then putting her back on a train certainly won't help. Between you and Luba—" He gestured toward the woman at the fire. "Bea will have better care than money could provide. I'll return in just a few days, I promise."

Dani said something else, but Beatrice couldn't make out her words. She'd become enchanted by the little pile of snowflakes on the window. It reminded her of the hill behind her grandmother's house in Minnesota where Papa had first taken her sledding. It seemed she was there, on his lap, with his arms around her. They were at the top of the mound, with the white world spread before them, rimmed by a brilliant blue sky. She could hear her father whoop with joy as he pushed off and they started down the slope, slow at first, but then picking up speed until they were flying through the air.

They landed with a whoosh of cold snow against her face and a thump that woke her. Again, she looked around. This time, she felt as though she'd been asleep for a long *time. Faint memories of Dani and the other woman, Luba, floated through her mind. Like muted scenes from a play, she saw them coax her to sip small spoonfuls of broth. They wiped her forehead and arms with cool cloths and slid ice across her sore lips.*

She felt a cool breeze on her cheeks and realized the thump came from the door to the little hut opening and then shutting against the blowing wind outside. The room was almost dark. Glowing embers from the fire cast a dim, shadowy light. She thought she saw movement.

And then Dani spoke. Her voice was soft and breathless. "Howard, you've been gone so long. I was worried."

No response.

"Howard?"

Beatrice saw her father stumble to the table and collapse into one of the chairs. "He never came. No one ever came to collect the crates."

Dani appeared beside him. "You sound exhausted. What did you do?"

He groaned. "What could I do? I waited as long as I could without arousing suspicion, but after I had everything loaded and ready to go, I couldn't stay with no good reason to be there. So I came back."

Silence. "You came back? You mean, you came back with the gold?"

Beatrice wondered why Dani sounded so scared.

"Howard!" Now she was angry. "How could you?"

"What else could I do?" His voice was harsh. "I couldn't very well leave it there, could I?" He glanced at his daughter and smiled. "Look, Beatrice is awake. How is she doing?"

"She comes and goes, but she's not really here. She's not

well, love." Dani took his hand and gasped. "And neither are you, Howard. You're burning up!"

When Beatrice opened her eyes again, her father was shivering on a pallet next to hers. Dani laid a cloth on his forehead, but he weakly pushed it away. "I'm fine. Take care of Bea."

"Papa?" Beatrice whispered.

He turned his head and smiled at her. "Ah, there's my girl. Now, Bea, listen to me." He touched her cheek. "Are you listening?"

"Yes, Papa." It was hard to speak, as if she hadn't done it for a very long time.

"You have to get better, so we can go home. Promise me, Bea." He ran his tongue across cracked lips. "Promise Papa you'll get better."

She nodded. "I promise."

He smiled and closed his eyes. "Good girl." And then they slept.

When Beatrice next opened her eyes, she saw Dani leaning over Howard, her head close to his. They were whispering softly to each other.

"I'm so sorry, Dani," Howard said. "You were right. We never should have come. I just thought...well...duty and country and all that." He coughed a deep, rasping cough. "Please get Beatrice back home. William is based at the American International headquarters in Yokohama. Call him when you arrive, and he'll find you a ship bound for San Francisco. Cable Mother when you reach Yokohama. She'll meet you in Seattle."

Beatrice heard him struggle for breath. She wanted to tell him she loved him and wanted to be with him, not her grandmother. But she was too weak to move or speak.

[192]

"I'm sorry to ask this of you," Howard whispered, "but if anyone can get my daughter back to America, it's you, Dani. You're the finest woman I've ever known. I love you. I always have. I'm sorry I didn't do right by you."

"Shhh..." Dani shook her head and wiped away tears, her tears, from Howard's cheeks. "I made my own choices, love." She chuckled softly. "Anything's better than boredom."

Much later, Beatrice opened her eyes and felt completely awake for the first time in days. Sunlight poured through the little window. The snowy hill on the glass had melted—and Papa was gone.

Alise stopped. Michael saw tears in her eyes. He had so many questions, but his wife wasn't concerned about details right then.

She smiled at him through her tears. "Silly," she said, wiping them away. "It was so long ago...and I never knew Howard or Dani. Gram wasn't at all emotional when she talked about her father's death. But it was like we were there in that awful, strange dream-world none of them could escape."

Michael moved to the couch and pulled Alise into the warmest embrace he could manage. Finally, he asked. "What happened next?"

She sniffed and returned to her corner. "Well, somehow, Dani got the two of them back to the States. Gram doesn't remember much of it. She was recovering from smallpox, which should have killed her, after all. She recalls being on a small vessel that took them from Vladivostok to Yokohama. I think she remembers it because it was filled with wounded Japanese soldiers plus at one point they thought it was going to sink. But they made it there, and then they boarded a cargo ship headed to Seattle."

"You'd think," Michael said carefully, "Dani could have booked them more luxurious accommodations. I mean, what happened to the gold?"

Alise shrugged. "Apparently, the gold never made it out of Chita. Dani and Luba were afraid to be caught with it. People were being assassinated right and left for much less in those days. Supposedly, the women buried the gold with Howard's body."

"Buried?" he said. "In Chita?"

"Gram didn't say. I don't know if she knows. But that was when she asked me to find the letter. I've read it many times, though, and it doesn't say anything important. Howard wrote the letter to his mother, and it mostly just talks about Beatrice—how smart she was, how she got along with everyone, what a good little traveler she was, stuff like that. Could be why Great-Grandma Ione gave it to her."

Michael knew the letter. He'd read it, and it was exactly as Alise described, with no valuable information and nothing that appeared to be code, although the writing was odd. The words were spaced erratically, making the page appear to have partial columns with rows running through it. Except for Beatrice's name in bold, capital letters in the very middle of the missive, the letter was written in perfect italic script.

He took a sip of tepid coffee. "Has your grandmother ever told you why she stopped going by the name Beatrice?"

Alise nodded. "That was Dani's doing. She couldn't figure out how to explain to the customs people in their ports of call why she was traveling alone with a child who was not her own. Back then, children didn't need passports, and under the circumstances, Dani apparently thought it was better to create a persona for Gram that had nothing to do with Howard and his exploits.

"She told everyone Gram was her daughter, so Gram left the country as a little white girl named Beatrice Viola Dickenson and returned as a bi-racial girl named Elena Sisk. Her Grandmother Ione kept the name to ensure Gram's mother never found her, although there is no evidence she ever tried to find her daughter. Eventually, Elena turned into Elaine, and that's the name that stuck."

"Why Elena?" Michael's training constrained him from leaving any question unanswered.

Alise smiled. "Dani told her Elena was the name of her best friend when she was a child in India. She said it meant 'Bright One.'"

———————

The Grandmother turned the letter over and held it up to the light. "Do you see it?" She was obviously excited, but what did she expect Alise to see?

Michael frowned and wished he had a better view. But he knew the words were even less visible than when he'd first read the letter. Was Alise supposed to be read the words backward? He'd already tried that.

Alise squinted at the paper. "Gram...?" He could tell she was barely containing her frustration. "I don't see anything but the words on the other side of the paper."

Elaine squirmed impatiently in her recliner. "No, no, dear." She pulled a well-worn rectangle of paper from the box the letter had come in. "It's not the words, it's the space *between* the words." She held the other piece of paper behind the letter, between it and the lamp.

Alise moved in closer and a surprised exclamation escaped her lips. Michael zoomed the camera focus and recognized the second piece of paper Elaine held as a section of a map of Old Chita. It was thin and linen-like, obviously much-handled, folded and re-folded.

With the map behind it, he could to see the letter was itself a map. The crazy columnar and horizontal spaces between the words perfectly overlaid and followed the streets of Old Chita.

Elaine smiled and told Alise "BEATRICE" was the X that marked the spot where her father was buried.

"So you've known all these years where Howard was buried?" Alise and Michael spoke at the same time, despite the distance and the camera between them. "But, Gram," Alise said, "how could Howard have written this if he was already dead?"

Elaine chuckled. "He didn't write it. Dani did. I wasn't lying to you. Those are his words, the exact words from the last letter he wrote before he died. But it's not in his hand. It's in Dani's. She made the map, so I would always remember where Papa was buried, so I could find him again, someday."

"Papa," Alise said softly, "and the gold."

Elaine shrugged, as if the gold was nothing. Michael thought briefly, but not seriously, *I should have killed her years ago.* "Well, yes, I suppose," she continued, "and the documents that proved his innocence. But that's not why I'm showing you this."

Alise sat back, a bemused expression on her face. "Well then, why? Why show me this now?"

[196]

"Because I want you to bury me with him."

"Gram..." Alise laughed, which she always did under stress. "What are you talking about? We're laying you to rest in the crypt with Mom and Grandpa Tobias and the great-grands. Your whole family is there, and I will be there, too, someday. It's what Grandpa wanted." She peered at her grandmother. "Remember how he used to smile when he talked about us all being together at the resurrection?" Alise started to rise from her seat as if the matter were closed.

Elaine grasped Alise by the arm in what was apparently a surprisingly strong grip. With a shocked cry, Alise fell back into the recliner.

"Listen, Alise..." Elaine's voice was urgent. "You've always been the strongest one of the family, even if you don't know it, and you've never let anyone down in your life. Don't you dare fail me now."

Alise rubbed her arm. "Strongest, except for you, you mean."

"I apologize, dear." Elaine patted her hand. "I didn't mean to hurt you. But you need to understand how important this is to me. Tobias was a sentimental old fool, and it's why I loved him. But all that rubbish about the resurrection...either we'll be together in heaven in a twinkling of an eye, or we won't. I hope and fervently believe it's the former, but there's nothing more I can do about it now."

A shadow crossed her face. "All these years, Papa has lain alone, unmarked, unremembered. And that's not right. You have to promise me, Alise, you'll take me to him. I loved him so much..." She stopped, seemingly at a loss as to how to make Alise understand the depth of her need.

"He saved me from a cold, northern, gray life. Mother was a hard woman who cared little for me beyond the work I could do. I would have been nothing more than a scullery maid in her boarding house, which was barely more than a house of ill repute, by the way. And he risked much to give me something else because he loved me."

Her voice grew stern. "That's what we do in this family, Alise. We risk everything for love. Papa wasn't perfect. He didn't always make the right choices. But he lived for things beyond himself. He lived for his family, for his country. And he lived as honorably as he could manage."

She grasped Alise's arm again. "I need you—and Michael—to stand at his grave and remember him for who he was. My papa was the first person to show me what real love was, and I left him behind, all these years. Help me make it right, Alise. It's my dying wish."

Alise started to say something, but Elaine wasn't finished. She raised her voice. "Think about Michael."

Alise looked puzzled. "What could Michael possibly have to do with this?"

"You're his life, Alise. You could never leave him, could you? That would be like leaving a part of yourself behind. And Michael, he would never leave you. He would do anything to keep you with him, because he knows he can't survive without you."

Michael pulled away from the screen, startled. But he shouldn't have been surprised. She'd always been one step ahead of him. She missed nothing. He'd known this from the beginning. But, still, as he heard those words crackle through the speakers, as he paused the picture, freezing the triumphant look on her face turned full at the camera, he was astounded by her boldness, her courage. She'd known who he was all along—and now she was letting him in on the joke that had so often made her eyes sparkle when he came into view.

———————

Alise was quiet, her head against his shoulder. Without speaking, they watched the train's shadow flow and ripple across the stubbled fields of the Russian countryside. Although an autumn sun followed their journey, the temperatures were already bitterly cold. Yet, Michael could tell, even after all these years abroad, that they would beat the winter's snows to Chita.

He thought back to Elaine's final days. Shortly after her conversation with Alise, the one in which she'd finally extracted a promise her ashes would be scattered on her father's grave, Michael pulled up a chair beside her bed. Alise was downstairs in the kitchen, preparing dinner. "Have you always known?" he asked, without preamble.

She'd been confined to her bed for days. The excitement of revealing the secret she'd hidden for so long seemed to have consumed what little life remained in her frail body. She laid very still, eyes closed. But then she smiled.

"Always," she said softly. "I knew the day you started watching me, just as I knew when your predecessor came and went."

"And my relationship with Alise? You encouraged it. I may not be as smart as you, Elaine, but that's one thing I'm sure about."

She shifted on her pillow. "You know what they say—keep your friends close, and your enemies... Besides, I liked you, Michael, and I knew you'd fall in love with her.

Who wouldn't? She's…"

"Amazing," he finished, without thinking.

Elaine opened her eyes and in them was her old smile. "Yes," she said. "But I don't understand why you needed her. Every conversation must have been recorded."

"You've become very good over the years at saying things without actually saying them, haven't you, Elaine? Alise helped me read between the lines."

She thought about that. Finally, she nodded.

"How do you know I won't leave her now?" he asked. "You must realize this is what we've been waiting for all this time."

Elaine set her jaw, and their eyes locked. She shrugged. "I *don't* know. But what can it matter now? I can't be the only reason you're here."

"No." He shook his head slowly. "I make…other connections."

"Is there even anyone who still remembers me?"

"My handler in London—"

"And he would notice if you just mentioned, casually, that I'd passed away? He doesn't have more important things to think about?"

It was a rhetorical question. She was obviously sure of the answer, and Michael was even more sure she was right.

"Besides," she continued, "it's a lot of money, yes. But to the great Empire of Russia? A drop in the bucket."

Michael's turn to smile. She didn't know all his secrets. "What makes you think I'm Russian?" He lifted an eyebrow as her eyes widened, as she began to understand. "Dozens of nationalities were recruited into the Secret

Service. When the USSR dissolved, many of them returned to their homes and took with them the secrets they'd learned. For some of those governments in the early 1900s, and for factions within those governments, the stash would have been enough to take over a country. Can you imagine what that gold would be worth today?" He grinned. "Maybe I'm British, or American. They know about the gold, too. Or maybe I just want it for myself."

"Luba probably dug it up after we left," she said smugly. "There's no way she, or some member of her family wouldn't have eventually succumbed to that kind of temptation."

"They weren't the only Russians who knew about the gold." Michael crossed his arms. "The one who initiated the whole scheme eventually came looking for it. Regretfully, it appears Luba and her family didn't survive the, uh, search."

For just a moment, Michael allowed himself to gloat. He held information she hadn't thought of. But the feeling soon soured. He'd grown to admire The Grandmother too much to enjoy the look of uncertainty in her eyes. His victory was short-lived, anyway.

"Alise doesn't need any gold," Elaine said, matter-of-factly. "I've left her everything. You'll both live very comfortably for the rest of your lives. You could never get that gold out without exposing yourself—and her—to danger."

She paused. "You've spent too much of your life wandering around the maze of her psyche, insinuating yourself into her heart, into both our hearts, and now you're stuck. You thought to trap us, Michael, but you're the one who's trapped, and you know it."

"You seem awfully sure of yourself."

She chuckled. "No, no. It's not me I'm sure of. It's love. There is no other viable option. Now," she said, suddenly all business, "I've answered all the questions. Your turn to help me. Please tell me they gave you something to make my death quick and painless."

Michael nodded, and she breathed a deep sigh of relief. "Thank God."

"Quick, painless *and* untraceable," he said. "But Alise would never forgive me. You know that."

"Would she need the details?" Her voice was weakening.

He considered that thought, but in the end, it was no good. He couldn't bring himself to create one more secret he had to keep from Alise, not even to spare The Grandmother pain.

She sighed, resigned. "Will you tell her who you really are?"

"She doesn't know? You haven't told her?" Michael searched The Grandmother's face, hoping beyond hope his secret was safe.

She moved her head back and forth against the pillow. "I've not told her, and I won't. But you can't discount the fact she has Dickenson blood in her veins. We don't miss much."

"I think," Elaine continued, her voice as feeble as her face was pale, "Alise knows you love her, and that's all she really cares to know. My question is how *much* do you love her?"

He leaned forward. "What do you mean?"

Elaine made an irritated sound. "Oh, Michael, for a spy,

you see so little. Is it too much for me to ask for a great-grandchild out of all this? It's the least you could do for us."

He grinned. "We'll see." The vision of a very different life than he'd ever dreamed could exist for him and Alise was still materializing. He was no longer sure he controlled any part of their future.

"*You* see to it, Michael," Elaine responded in a stronger, cowboy-up tone of voice. "I'm done." She turned her head and closed her parchment-thin lids. Soon, she appeared to be sleeping contentedly—and true to her word, she was done.

———————

Speeding on a train toward an unmarked grave at the edge of a cemetery in Old Chita, Michael thought about how quiet he and Alise were with each other now. He had no more reason to question her, and she seemed happily lost in her own thoughts. Anything but boredom? *Anything?*

He could dig up the gold, which was what he'd prepared his entire adult life to do. He didn't need his handler in London. He knew whom to call. He had names and numbers from the old days. They would put him in touch with the right people. Even though everyone else had forgotten, when the story was told, he would be hailed as a hero—in a home he no longer knew.

Yet, to fulfill his mission, he'd have to leave Alise behind, which would most likely mean her death. She knew too much. He closed his eyes. The Grandmother, as usual, was right. There was no life without this blond head on his shoulder, these fingers entwined in his.

He said her name softly. "Alise..."

"Yes?"

"What are you thinking about?"

When she didn't answer, he wondered if she'd heard him. But then she lifted her head, looked into his eyes and smiled. "I was thinking about children."

———————

SPIRIT OF CHRISTMAS

Rebecca Carey Lyles

"Ah, Christmas Eve." Jack Wymore loosened his tie, kicked off his shoes and settled into the couch cushions next to his wife.

Carol snuggled close. "The kids thought this night would never come."

He wrapped his arms around her and rubbed his day's-end chin stubble over her soft auburn hair. Soothed by her nearness and the sound of logs crackling in the fireplace, he felt the tension of a long and hectic day begin to drain away. From the minute the store opened until it closed, the aisles had been jam-packed with last-minute shoppers who'd apparently left their Christmas joy at home.

Seated on the floor in front of a fake tree dripping with tinsel, six-year-old Suzy began their family's traditional Christmas Eve reading from the Gospel of Luke. She slid her chubby finger across the page in rhythm with her speech, reading one word at a time. "In...those...days..."

Bobby, Suzy's older brother, pounded the carpet with his fist. "I can't believe you're letting her read, Mom. She reads so slow, we'll *never* get to open presents."

Carol sat up. "How many times have I told you not to exaggerate?"

Jack sighed. He should have known the tranquility wouldn't last.

"We just went to church." Bobby folded his arms. "Isn't that enough religion for one night?"

"Hush, so your sister can read."

Bobby glowered at his mother but said nothing more.

Suzy bent over the Bible again. "I lost my place."

"That's okay. You'll find it." Carol lifted two steaming mugs from the coffee table and handed one to Jack.

He breathed in the rich aroma of the spiced cider before he raised the cup to his lips. As he sipped, he gazed beyond the glittering tree framed by their living room's picture window. Snowflakes shimmered around the street lamp that illuminated their snowy street, and lights twinkled on the roof of the house across the way.

Like a scene from a Christmas card, knee-deep snow enveloped their neighborhood in silent solitude. Peace settled on Jack like a warm quilt. No phones, no cars. Even the neighbor's yapper was quiet. And... He chuckled to himself. His meddling mother-in-law's plane was grounded in Chicago.

"I found where I was," Suzy said. "Quir, Quir–in..."

Bobby's freckles flared. "Just skip it and go to the next word."

"Bobby..." Carol gave him a stern look and then smiled at Suzy. "That's *Qurinius*, sweetie."

Jack glanced from the living room to the dining room. For the first time, he noticed the elaborate decorations. Holly, mistletoe, bells and stars hung in windows and doorways. Silver and gold garland wove between angels and snowmen on the fireplace mantle, and a red platter stacked with homemade goodies rested on the coffee table in front of him.

He pulled Carol close and whispered in her ear, "Nice work."

She frowned. "Huh?"

He swept his hand across the room. "The decorations."

She raised an eyebrow. "They've been up since Thanksgiving."

"Shhh," demanded Suzy. "And every...everyone..."

He set his mug down to reach for an obviously kid-decorated sugar cookie. *Should have kept my mouth shut.* Carol hated the long hours he put in during the holidays and how he kept the store open as late as possible on Christmas Eve. He bit into the cookie. She was especially ticked he'd missed the candlelight service at church, again.

But... He chewed and swallowed. *She doesn't mind the money. It was her idea to buy Bobby that ridiculously expensive—*

"Na–za–reth," Suzy stammered in her high voice, her head bent in concentration and her blonde pigtails falling onto the Bible. Jack smiled at his determined little girl. She'd been so eager to read the Christmas story this year, despite Bobby's objections.

"Cut it out, Bobby," Carol had chided. "I think it's sweet

she wants to participate at such a young age."

In response, Bobby stuck his finger in his mouth and made gagging noises.

Jack watched his chunky son inch his largest gift from behind the tree, ready to rip as soon as his sister finished. Bobby had always chafed at the delay in opening gifts, no matter who read the scripture passage. Jack smiled a wry smile. *Christmas—nothin' like it.* He picked up his cider to wash down the dry cookie.

Bobby helped Suzy pronounce *Bethlehem.* "Come on, Suz. Pl-ease don't go so slow—"

Carol shook a finger at him. "This story is what Christmas is all about. You get your greedy little paws off that package and listen."

Suzy droned on. "He be–longed..."

Jack caressed his wife's shoulder. *I wonder what Carol got me. She won't even let me touch that big blue package in the back. Maybe it's a*—

The doorbell rang.

Jack jerked, spilling hot cider on himself, Carol and the couch. "God da—" He clamped his teeth together. "Who in the world?"

Carol jumped to her feet. "Someone sure has nerve. Don't they know it's Christmas Eve?" She dabbed at her slacks with a napkin.

Setting his cup on the coffee table, he wiped his hands on his pants and stood.

Carol grabbed his arm. "You don't have to answer it."

"Might be a last-minute delivery."

She arched her eyebrows. "At this hour?"

"I bet it's the paper boy," Suzy declared. "Collecting."

"Yeah." Bobby slipped his fingers under the fold at the end of the package. "He just wants more of Mom's fudge."

"Shhh." Carol put her finger to her lips. "He already collected for December."

The bell rang again. Jack pulled his arm out of his wife's grasp and moved toward the entryway.

"For Pete's sake," she hissed. "It's Christmas Eve. Whoever it is ought to know better than to interrupt our celebration. They'll go away."

"What if someone needs help or is having car trouble. It's cold out there."

"Jack..." Her green eyes chilled to steel-gray. "You always think of everyone else but us. Is once a year too much to ask? This is *our* time. The kids will have a fit if they have to wait to open gifts while you're out playing mechanic again. As it is, we started late because you stayed at the store so long."

"Yeah," Bobby and Suzy chorused.

The bell rang again.

Carol returned to her spot on the couch, but Jack remained standing.

Suzy found her place. "Ex–pec–ting a child..."

Bobby rotated the box and slid his finger through the other end of the wrapping.

Tapping the couch cushion, Carol said, "Sit down, Jack. They'll leave."

"I..."

"It's okay. They'll understand."

He started for the kitchen. "Better find something to clean that spot before it dries."

The doorbell rang again.

Jack stood in the middle of the living room, looking from the entryway to Carol and back again.

"Dad, please," Bobby whined. "*Please* sit down."

Jack hesitated. Finally, he walked over to a chair and sat. Seated on the edge of the cushion, hands clasped between his knees, he stared at the entry.

The fire sputtered and popped.

And, again, the bell chimed, even louder than before. At least that's how it sounded to Jack.

Bobby swore.

Carol glared at him. "No more of that, young man."

Suzy continued. "The time came...for the baby..."

Jack got to his feet. "I can't take it."

Despite his family's groans, he opened the door. A hint of warmth and a spark of sunshine colored the breeze that blew through the screen door. He didn't know what the aroma was that accompanied the swirl of spring air, but it was better than anything he'd ever smelled before. Jack switched on the porch light and saw a solitary man wearing simple but warm clothing.

The stranger smiled. "Hello."

"Hello." Jack glanced toward the curb.

"That's right. No car." The man grinned. "I'm Jesus Christ. I don't usually drive one." He lifted a gloved hand. "I'd like to celebrate Christmas with your family this year."

Jack recoiled. *Jesus? Impossible. Absurd.*

"Dad, hurry up!"

Jack gaped at the visitor, whose open gaze seemed to radiate love, compassion, joy, peace, mercy, truth—and so much more. He saw a depth in the man's eyes he knew he could never fathom.

[210]

"May I come in?" The stranger's smile was warm and inviting.

Jack heard Carol's voice. "Close the door, Jack. You're letting in the cold."

"I, uh, well, you see—we're right in the middle of reading the...uh, actually—your story in the Bible, and—"

"Come on, Dad. We've got to get this religion stuff over with."

Jack grimaced. *Maybe he's come to preach at us. Bobby will have a fit.*

"No," Jesus said. "I'm here to celebrate with you." He winked. "Like you've never celebrated before."

"I've got to consider my son. You see, he's at that age." Jack cleared his throat. "I mean, everything has to be, you know, cool. And my wife—she, Carol, she really wants just the family to be together tonight. It so rarely happens..."

"Da-ad!"

"I understand." Jesus stepped away but stopped and turned back. His eyes were filled with tender pain. "I love you."

"I, uh, love ya, too. Maybe—maybe next year would be a, you know,   better time for you to visit."

"Maybe." Jesus descended the steps to trudge through a walkway buried in deep, heavy snow.

Jack watched the bowed figure slog into a swirl of snowflakes then disappear in the darkness. A terrible emptiness flooded his soul, and a shiver shook his body. He shoved the screen door open to call him back.

But Carol was tugging at his arm. "Good grief, Jack. You're going to give us all pneumonia." She pulled him inside the house, turned off the porch light and closed the door behind them.

"What did that man want?" Suzy asked, once again bent over the Bible, and once again searching for her spot.

"Oh..." Jack sighed. "Not much. He was just hoping he could celebrate with us."

Bobby snorted and loosened the final piece of tape.

Carol rolled her eyes. "Can you believe it? Christmas, no less."

"Here it is." Suzy began to read again. "Be–cause there...was no...room..."

Down the street, around the corner, another doorbell rang.

———————

ACKNOWLEDGEMENTS

Lisa Michelle Hess graciously served as the assistant editor for *Passageways*. Her insights were amazing and her attention to detail, whether she was working with content, interior design or cover design, helped create a quality final product. Lisa is a delightful lady and a fun, kind critique partner. Lunch is on me, Lisa.

With great gratitude, we thank our eagle-eyed proofreaders—Steve Lyles, Kathy Schuknecht, Alissa Ketterling and Jim Ketterling—who went beyond the call of duty to suggest changes that enhanced our writing. You made us look good! And, yes, you're invited to lunch, too.

ABOUT THE AUTHORS

Valerie D. Gray has finished her first young-adult novel, a time-travel mystery, and is now in the rewriting process, aiming for 2015 publication. She and her husband of 38 years, Bill Gray, gladly claim the title "trailing grandparents." Several years ago, they followed their two daughters and their families from California to Boise, Idaho, where they all now reside. valeriegray.com

Lisa Michelle Hess is a literary fiction and non-fiction author and blogger, journalist, Christian non-profit consultant, mentor of women, homeschooling mom and a thoroughly Pacific Northwest girl. Her writing has appeared in numerous publications over the years. She is currently living in Boise, Idaho, and completing her first full-length novel. lisamichellehess.com

Peter Leavell, a 2007 graduate of Boise State University with a degree in history, was the 2011 winner of Christian Writers Guild's Operation First Novel contest, and 2013 Christian Retailing's Best award for First-Time Author. His published works include "Gideon's Call," a Civil War novel, and "God & Gun," a Dakota Territory western. Peter and his family live in Meridian, Idaho. peterleavell.com

Rebecca Carey Lyles grew up in Wyoming, the setting for her award-winning Kate Neilson novels, "Winds of Wyoming" and "Winds of Freedom." She now lives in Idaho, where she serves as an editor and a mentor for aspiring authors and women transitioning from prison to life "on the outside." She's also writing the third book in the "Winds" series. beckylyles.com

http://www.perpedit.com